Twice Born

The Paranormal Canadiana Collection

Graeme Smith

Print ISBNs

Amazon print 9780228636816
Ingram Spark 9780228636823
Barnes & Noble 9780228636830
BWL Print 9780228636847

Copyright 2025 Graeme Smith
Editor Gail Branan
Cover artist Michelle Lee

Forward

This is a Fantasy. Parts of it involve partial descriptions of rituals and, for want of a better word, magic.

It's all lies.

Er—no. I don't mean magic is all lies. Or that it isn't. That's a discussion for another day. But the rituals? Er—don't. I mean it. I'm a fiction author, which means I'm a professional liar. So either I have no idea what the rituals really are, so I'm making it all up, or I know what they are, or think I do, and I'm lying. Don't try them. Really.

While we're on the subject—magic. Which is or isn't real, depending on your beliefs. But this book involves 'real' things, so there's that. But before we begin all 'that', let's get some terms straight. Terms which have been used (and still are) in real history. Like witches. Whatever Hollywood, or anything else, told you, witches can be male witches, female witches, and every other gender in between. Anything else is just a load of warlocks. Er—I mean nonsense. Mikumwessuk (we'll get to Mikumwessuk, don't worry) are like that too. Male and female. And maybe witches too, Benandanti, or maybe something else entirely. And witches aren't sorcerers. Witches have their own innate power, part of their nature from birth, or given to them. Sorcerers don't have any power, but they have learned ways to manipulate the power around them using rituals and 'magic words'. Think of it like flying. Birds can fly because of themselves. Pilots can fly because they know how to use a 'magic wand'—a plane—to achieve the same thing.

And then there's skin-walkers. In this case, wolf skin-walkers. With apologies to Lon Chaney, not everything that sometimes looks like a wolf and sometimes like something else is a howling monster, but only at full moons. There are groups (the Mi'kmaq, the Benandanti in Northern Italy are only two of many) who believe that wolves, and wolf skin-walkers, are allies in their guardianship of the land. And skin-walkers don't have to wait for full moon either. The Benandanti even called wolves, and wolf walkers, 'soldiers of God'. Oh. And since it's in the prologue, there's Bruxas. A Bruxa is a witch. Sort of. The Bruxas (or Cogas), in Sardinian traditions, are witches with the appearance of an old woman, having the ability to assume any shape and size both animal and vegetable or even of people. During the night, in groups or alone, they sneaked into houses to kill male babies. To protect their children, the parents placed a cane rod and a blessed rosary on the baby's cradle. When the witches arrived next to the cradle they began to count the beads of the rosary, without ever being able to count them all before dawn, when they were forced to flee so as not to be hit by the sunlight. The Bruxas looked like old women but they recognized each other mainly because they had a small piece of tail since they were born and could take on any shape. In some versions of their story the Bruxas are vampires, who get their blood (and eternal life and power) from the young they kill.

I would also like to acknowledge the help I have been given by Andrew Maclean, of radio television and print fame–the author of the New Brunswick 'Backyard History' books. I am sure I have made many mistakes in this book, but many I could have made were not-made because of his assistance. Thanks Andrew!

I'll say up front, there are a number of words and phrases here that aren't English. The languages fit the context, at least I believe so, but Appendix 1 has them translated, and sorted by Chapter.

Apologies

What follows is intended as a tale. It is a work of fiction. However, like any work of fiction, or almost any perhaps, it involves elements from the world often called more 'real'. So it starts in Italy. And starting in Italy, it involves elements of Italian history, of language and of, for want of a better word, folklore. But it doesn't stay in Italy, because this is also a tale of Canada—more specifically, of New Brunswick. And, in a sense, of more than that, because it involves elements of a people who were here long before any European, Italian or otherwise, set foot here. Of the Mi'kmaq. And so it also involves elements of history, of lore and legend and, yes, of tales from Canada, from New Brunswick and, yes, from Mi'kmaq culture.

And that, potentially, is something for which I feel I must apologise.

I am not Italian. And while I am Canadian, and while I live in New Brunswick, I was not born here. I did not grow up with the history, the language and, yes, the lore and legends of any of the places found in this book. And so, I guarantee, there will be errors.

Those errors are entirely mine, and I apologise for them unreservedly.

While I have tried to be diligent in my research, still, those errors will be here. And not just errors. For example, the Mi'kmaq culture has tales of what might be known as dragons (referred to as Jipijka'm, Chepechcalm and Tcipitckaam), as in, for example, the tale of the Magic Dancing Doll. And if a dragon appeared in this book (no spoilers), should I put one of those tales here? Well, consider this. While I have read that in Mi'kmaq culture there is no single owner of oral lore or tales, I have also read of a Maine historian, Dena Winslow, who worked for the Aroostook Band. She said that "a story told by a Mi'kmaq storyteller belongs to the storyteller and cannot be retold unless the storyteller gifts you that story. If you receive a story as a gift, you'll know it." And I have never been gifted any Mi'kmaq tales. But still, the people called Mi'kmaq in New Brunswick are here in this tale. And for that I do not apologise, for they are more part of this land than any who arrived later.

Dedication

This is a book born of Canada—specifically New Brunswick. But a large part of Canada's story doesn't start in Canada. It starts 'away'. In places people leave for good reasons and bad, to escape and to find new homes, to grow and to learn—for many reasons. People who 'come from away'. And this book is no different. So this book is dedicated to all those who 'came from away'—and to my home. New Brunswick. A Canadian Province which is 80% trees, and much better for being so :-).

This book is also dedicated to my Evil Publisher, Lady Jude the very-not-obscure. Who sent me an email. And in Lady Jude's case, the pen isn't just mightier than the sword, it beats a 357 Magnum as well! And it's dedicated to Lady Gail, who put up with reading it (after I'd hypnotised her), and said it wasn't totally horrible. On the other hand, she's an author too, so she's a professional liar, just like me (blush). And this book is dedicated to my beloved wife, the ever-patient Crystal. And clearly ever-insane, since she married me (blushes again).

Acknowledgement

BWL Publishing acknowledges the Government of Canada and the Canada Book Fund for its financial support in creating the Canadian Historical Mysteries collection.

BWL Publishing acknowledges the Province of Alberta for their ongoing support through the Alberta Publisher's Cultural Industry Operating Grant.

*** The Paranormal Canadiana
Collection ***

Night at the Legislature – Manitoba – Author Nancy M. Bell

Shúhta Dene – Northwest Territories – author Maureen Gresl

Astraphobia – Saskatchewan – author Paul Grant

Dancing Mary – British Columbia – author Jay Lang Young

Twice born – New Brunswick – author Graeme Smith

Playtime – Prince Edward Island – author Eden Monroe

2026 Releases

Ghosts of Bell Island - Newfoundland - Eileen Charbonneau and Jude Pittman

Black Gold Eye - Alberta – author JD Shipton

Haunting the Klondike - Yukon – author Joan Donaldson-Yarmey

Cardinal - Nova Scotia – author donalee Moulton

The Deepest Divide - Ontario – JC Kavanagh

Metamorphe - Quebec – author Juliet Waldron with John Wisdomkeeper (posthumously)

Table of Contents

Prologue

Sit-rep–Once upon a time

ECSED CASTLE – another time

"Fewmets. I think I have something."

"Blood and dirt, Edward. I'm sorry. Did you manage to...?"

"No. Her Father came from the fields too soon."

The Supervisor shakes his head. "What do you have? If you're lucky, it's really nothing."

The young man shows his Supervisor the file he had been reading, one of many and many, and many more, all piled on the desks filling the room, clerks reading each of them in detail, in turn. The Supervisor reads it, noting the underlines Edward had put in place. "Well Edward. Well indeed. I think you're right. It has Him all over it. In other circumstances, this would be a promotion– the Countess wants him very, very badly. I'm–well, I'm sorry Edward. But you know the rules. Take it to her."

I shake my head. Fuck. Dad's good– heck, the best. Though if you ever tell him I said that, I'll kill you. Mind you, if you ever get to meet him, odds are he'll be there to kill you anyway. We do that a lot, we Shadows. I wrap the shadow shift tight round me and I follow Edward, whatever an Edward is. It would be the usual over-dramatic movie-villain castle, if it weren't for the fact that it was real. And in case you ever need to know, down is never a good direction in castles like that.

Yes. We go down.

Edward knocks at the door. As doors go it is big and imposing. And totally not locked. Which is also not good in such places. It means whoever is inside has no issues with anyone going in. Because them coming back out again is unlikely to be a problem. The sounds from within are a mixture of moans, fading screams and—yes. Splashing.

Dad had told me about this place. And how he'd handled it. Me, it wasn't a problem. Edward? Hmmmm....

Edward knocks again.

"Enter."

Edward knocks.

"I said enter, fool."

"Countess, I... I mean..."

"I. Said. Enter. To interrupt my bathing, you must believe you have something I wish to see. Enter."

"Countess, I... I mean... I am... I mean, I haven't..."

"Yes, fool. I know. I can smell it on you. Now enter. If you are correct in your belief, you might possibly leave again. If you are not? Then you will share my bath. NOW ENTER!"

Edward goes in. Shadow-wrapped, I follow. Erzsébet Bathory is indeed in her bath. The previous, um, let's say 'containers' of what she is sat in hang from the walls. She holds her hand out, dripping red. Edward wipes it with a towel, and passes her the papers. She reads them. Then she reads again. "Bassza meg! On my Mother's life, not that I ever liked the bitch. Yes. Yesssssss. A senior officer's extra-curricular activities in Whitechapel cease. The officer disappears, but his Tag does not trigger. And a mysterious, legless man appears from nowhere on a deserted beach. Oh, Jack, Jack, Jack. It is you. It is! I can smell it! I have you now, fattyú." She looks up. "You. Whoever you are."

"Ed... Edward, Countess."

She looks him up and down. "Interesting. You are either eternally stupid, or foolishly brave. To tell me your name, I mean. Let us find out. Tell your Supervisor you are to be promoted three grades. Which means, you either have Him brought to me in chains, or you will indeed share my bathing with me. Put together a team, and get it done. NOW."

I pull the shadows tight. As the Countess had said. Fuck. This isn't good. I don't need to get the file. I know where I have to be. Unicorn horn and virgin's tears— never be without it. I pull the bottle from my belt.

* * *

BAIE STE MARIE, NEW SCOTLAND – September 8th, 1863

A cold wind blew along the beach. The empty beach. At least until the shadows flex and shiver. I see Dad drop Jack from his shoulder. Prowess is with him. Who's Prowess? It doesn't matter. Well. She matters. But not here. That's another story. Lots of stories. Shape shifting, empathivore concert pianists are like that. But Prowess' smile is as cold as the wind, and then some. She looks at the body on the sand, the tar cold on its chopped legs. "So what do we do, Jack? He's empty now. You going to kill him?" Dad tells her about the Tag. How the Dragon will know if the other one dies. Told her how the Dragon would smell it on Dad if he killed him. Prowess frowns. "But—but he'll be dead anyway, won't he?"

I could see P's lips moving as she tried to work out how a guy who was going to have been dead for a hundred and fifty years wasn't going to be dead when they'd taken him from. And if that sounds confusing, you're right. It is. But that's not how it works. When you Tag someone, the Tag's in their head with them. Say I Tagged you yesterday, at Carnegie Hall, then took you some other time, some other year or day, century or minute. The Tag wouldn't know you were in the Back-Along, at least, Back-Along relative to when I tagged you. Just know a day was

18

gone and you weren't dead. But when you die? The Tag wouldn't know when. Just that it happened so many days after it was set on you. And I'd get a print of every soul near you the moment it happened. Actually, it isn't like that at all. But it's close enough.

Prowess shrugs. "So what do we do, Jack?"

Dad shrugs too. "Can you put anything in him? Anything at all?"

"There's always a bit left. A fragment. A scratch of his soul. So yes. A few words, maybe."

"Well then. Not Jack. Jason. John. Something beginning with J."

Prowess eyes look far away, across a distant horizon of years. "I knew a boy once. Jerome...."

"Where was that, P?"

Prowess smiles, her eyes still distant. "What? Oh. Trieste. But...." Her eyes focus back on the here and now. "But no matter." Her eyes focus on Jack. Not Dad-Jack, the other one, the one with no legs. "There. It's done." They turn to leave—but two shots ring out. Dad falls, and Prowess too. Dad used to have an emergency kit for a time like this. But he used it when I killed him. I mean, it wasn't me, but it was. That's another long story. I look at the six bodies round me, all suffering an overdose of my piano wire to the throat. Apparently the team Edward sent was eight. I had to fix it. Fix it before it happened. Because that's what we do, Dad and me. Fix things. Things that get messed up, then fix them before they mess. The Universe was going to take a little time getting over the shock of Dad being gone. So I have a chance, but not a great one. I pull the bottle from my belt.

* * *

350 FIFTH AVENUE AND DOWN – Some day

Sometimes, things can get on top of you. This time, it was Fifth Avenue. 350 Fifth Avenue, to be precise. 350 Fifth Avenue and one thousand four hundred and seventy two feet of straight-up. OK, plus the fifty five feet of straight-down foundation I was at the bottom of. No, they don't take the tours down there. They don't even know there's a 'down there' to take them to. Dad had paid someone a lot of money to make sure there was a down here nobody knew about. But I know. And I know it's the last place that will go if the Universe catches on to what happened. Now I lean against a wall that hadn't been touched since Dad built it in 1929. I have a job to do. I just don't know how to do it. Or rather, how I'd already done it. Dad would say that was a bugger. I don't. I say it's a question. And where there's a question, there's someone with an answer. Or sort-of someone.

"Look. Can you at least draw the bloody triangle? I am going to have *such* a migraine."

I grab some chalk. Dad always keeps—well, technically, right now always kept, but I was working on that, some chalk handy at 350. I draw the triangle, complete with sigils. No. I won't tell you which sigils. No. There wasn't blood. Or maybe there was—you want to summon demons, you draw your own bloody—or not bloody—mystical symbols. You know, all the books say there's supposed to be some sort of sign when someone who wasn't there before decides to be there. Which just shows what books know. Because there isn't a noise, or a crash of lightning, but he's there. If he hadn't been shaped like a man, he would have looked like a leopard. "You know, it's really rather fascinating. Of course, Jack will remember. Mostly because he, well because he can't remember." That's Hauras for you. Fallen Angel, Great Duke of Hell, Knower of all things past, present and future. Or not. One of those. Because he's more than that, though that's not for this tale. The leopard not-man stops. He shakes his head, his lips moving. I have a feeling he's repeating what he'd just said. He sighs. "Bugger. That doesn't even make sense even to me, and I know everything." He sighs again. "If I wasn't immortal, I swear you Shadows would be the bloody death of me. Ahem. Right. I see your problem. And it's a doozy. Your Father's former employers have their eyes on everyone there. You can't use any of them." Hauras winks. "You hear me? You use anyone, anyone who ever existed, and they'll be on to you. So we're clear, right? I told you it's impossible. Im-poss-i..." he pauses, winks "... bull." And he winks. Again. There isn't a crash of lightning, or a noise—but he's gone. Which is fine. Because he's not-told me all I need to know. I'm going to need help though. Charlie? Yeah. Charlie. Wherever it was, Charlie would have been there already. But Charlie might not listen to me. Or anyone else. Except for one—just one. So Rosie? Yeah. Rosie. Some local Talent, wherever local turned out to be. And maybe Katya and Darek to ride shotgun.

Damn. This was going to be fun! Or the end of the Universe. Or both. Like, again. Dad and I are like that.

Chapter 1

Twice born

FRIULI, ITALY – September 19th, 1835

There should have been thunder. There should have been lightning tearing the skies and the very heavens weeping. There should have been portents and comets and demons of fire riding skeletal horses of ice-white bone—but if there had been, this would have been a movie. Probably with very artistic lens flare. So there wasn't. What there was, was a small house. A small house in a small glen in the Southern Limestone Alps of Friuli, Italy. And yes. Friuli is a long, loooong way from Ne... but no. We'll get to that. And get there. But not yet. Spoilers, OK?

Ahem. Where was I? Oh. Right.

There was a house, small and lost in the little glen. There was a single window casting candle-light into the falling evening. Which was exactly how it was supposed to be. What was to come next? Not so pretty. But that's how it is, when you do what I do. You have to start somewhere nobody will ever miss, if you're going to make it different.

Ahem. Yes. Right. Stop talking May... I mean, stop talking.

On the hill above the house, a dark figure stood in the lee of the great oak there. And a single tear fell from my—I mean, like, *her*—eye. And the tear wasn't of blood. I mean, yeah. It *should* have been blood. Like, it would have been, like, really cool if it was. But it wasn't. So there. Ahem. And as the tear fell, she lifted her hand and caught it on a finger. And she looked at the drop of tear-that-wasn't-blood-but-should-have-been for a moment, then looked up at the moon and the stars and the sky-bowl... and she smiled a smile set in pain. Which I didn't. Me being me, I mean. And my job being... well, my job being what it is, I bloody didn't. But it's really cool and artistic. So pretend I did. Or pretend whoever *she* was did. Because it wasn't me, right?

And where the figure stood, shadows danced and twisted. And the figure knelt, and she pulled a wolf skin from the pack she wore. Or should that be bore? I mean, us being back in 1800 and change? I don't know. Wore, bore—well. Let's hope not bore. I'd hate to bore you. I'd probably have to kill you, just to keep my street cred. So anyway. I—I mean *she* pulled the wolf skin from her pack, and drew a blade from her belt. And I *know* the blade was inscribed with eldritch symbols, because I watched Waylan draw them myself. I just have no idea what 'eldritch' means. So she drew the knife and stabbed it through the wolf skin, pinning it to the old oak tree she stood under. Was standing under. Will stand under. Look, time shadowing is a bugger. It's one of those, OK? Then she pulled a bottle from her pocket. It would have gleamed red in the sunlight, being blood and all. But as we've established, it's falling evening. So no sun, right? And she opened the bottle, and drew more eldritch symbols on the wolf skin. And they glowed. Which was a really good thing, or I'd have had to go do some really not-good things to the one who'd told me how to draw them. Er—told *her*, I mean. Or try to–him being a nearly-not-quite-god-of-Smiths and all.

So we have the cottage. Which is a good start. And nobody in the cottage weeping. Which, in a different world, maybe they should have been. But not this world. And not this cottage. The woman not-weeping had a reason to be weeping, but she wasn't doing it. What my Leupold BX-4 Pro Guide HD binoculars (yes, I know. Year 1800 and change. Remember that whole 'time shadowing' thing I mentioned?) told me she *was* doing, was opening her door and coming out of the cottage. And in low light, you can't beat a pair of Leupold BX-4s. I could see them. The placenta. The umbilical cord. Which meant—yes. The bottle. Birth blood, mixed with grappa I'd bet would have had to move up town to even know what a bathtub was, but would be sixty per-cent proof if it was even trying. And a burning stick. Then the woman, she puts down a mess of kindling, and she puts the placenta on it and the umbilical cord. And she dances round the pile widdershins, which is counter to the sun's course, or anti-clockwise if you don't have some of the friends—or the not-friends—I do. And she's muttering something to herself. All of which, if she only knew, was a total waste of time. She dances three times, then she stops, shouts something she probably thought was esoteric, pours the bottle on kindling and co., then throws the burning stick on it. The huge flame leaping up is fairly normal. The bird that swoops down and transforms into a bent over old woman is normal too—but only if you live in my world, and not yours. Then the bitch from the cottage bows to the old, bent woman, opens her door and ushers her in. Which makes her, local puttana with bad-for-business-issue or not, a whole lot more bitchy. But exactly the reason I'm here. So I wait. I wait until the Bruxa comes out of the door, and runs off as a rabbit. Then I, I mean, like, the girl on the hill, she starts down into the glen. But half way down, she stops. Because I nearly bloody forgot. So I put on the ring, and the girl isn't a girl anymore. She's a Mikumwessuk. You say it like 'mee-kum-oo-wess-uk'. Which wouldn't mean a thing in Friuli. But it would to the Mi'kma... well, I mean to some other people in some other place we haven't got to yet. The Mikumwessuk are little people, like dwarves or fairies. They're generally OK forest spirits (because there's a lot of forest in Ne… in where they live, I mean), but they can be really kick-ass dangerous if they're disrespected. Anyway, girl? No. Mikumwessuk? Yes. And she doesn't knock, because when you're what she is, you don't knock at human doors, especially to the kind of bitch who's inside this door. But, like they say, it's always good to make an entrance. So I touch—I mean *she* touches—the door. And it explodes open. Amazing what a little tiny blasting cap on your finger can do. She goes in, and she goes over to the not-crying woman by the bed. She looks down, and she stands in silence. Because, like, it's more impressive and commanding that way. She looks down, but not at the puttana who hadn't taken care of not having business interruptions. She looks down at the small, silent body lying in the bitch's bed. A body still red from birthing, but not a breath in him, with a rag stuffed over his face and in his mouth. So the Mikumwessuk, she looks down. And she scribes some more eldritch, whatever eldritch is, in the red blood on the dead boy's skin. Which is really not important. What is important is the cut she makes on the dead boy's thigh with something that just shouldn't cut it—a small emerald that she slips inside the cut. A cut which closes and seals without a trace left behind. Then she takes the part-full bottle from her pocket, opens it, pulls the rag away and puts it to the dead boys lips. Which would have been kind of dumb, him being dead and all, but turned out to be kind of not dumb, since he drank. And even though nobody could see it (because I'm damn good at what I do, and only my Dad is better, but if you tell him I said so I really *will* kill you), up the hill, the wolf skin dagger-ed to the tree disappears, and the dagger falls to the ground. And it vanished, because it wasn't that dagger's time yet. And I look at the puttana-bitch, and I say "You touch one hair on his head, and I will find you. And you will wish the Bruxa had taken *you*." And I look down at the boy. "You owe me. And I *always* make sure my debts are paid. Remember that." Then I turn round, and I walk out of the door. Because, like, *drama,* you know? And I, I mean, whoever the girl was, she walks up the hill. At the top, I turn and look down at the cottage. Because this is where it begins. The only plan I have to get Dad back. Or rather, to make sure I never have to get him back in the first place. Something like that. Which is when it happens. Because someone taps me on my shoulder. Which *never* happens, because *nobody* can sneak up on me. I spin round, my Glock in my hand, and he's there. He's there, and he bows, and he stands up, and he's doing it. He's bloody smiling! And he says it. The thing he can't possibly say. He says "Ciao, Mamma." I mean, Mamma? Fuck. Like, as in, what-the. Because this? This wasn't in the plan. And I know I can pull the trigger on my

Glock—but I know I can't. Because I see. I see what's in his hand.

* * *

There should have been thunder. There should have been lightning tearing the skies and the very heavens weeping. There should have been portents and comets and demons of fire riding skeletal horses of ice-white bone—and possibly even lens flare. There wasn't. But on a hill above the glen more than the tree—waited.

Chapter 2

Thrice named

FRIULI, ITALY – September 19th, 1845

Moccio. That's what she called him from the first he could ever remember. Not on the rare occasions they were round people. People who might talk, anyway. People who could sully even a puttana, and ruin her business. Oh no. Then? Then he got to be 'Ellerimo'. With others? With her 'callers'? With those even she could call friends? Moccio. The yucky green that oozed down from a Winter nose. But even that—it wasn't his name. His real name. Strega moccioso. That's what she would yell at him, before she hit him for some made-up transgression, her face bright red and her eyes glaring. And then the blows. A slap, a fist—a bundled set of birch twigs. And even then, only to hide what she was the other times. The times she thought he could not hear her, did not know. The times she would whisper it, when it wasn't any anger in her eyes, but rather stark fear. 'Strega moccioso', and a quick sign of the cross over her heart. Or signs that were

30

no cross at all but still, he knew, her ward against him.

Strega moccioso. Witch spawn.

But Ellerimo or Moccio—or the other name, that only they two knew—she still found work for him. Schools were for rich folk, of which there were few near their cabin, and he for sure not one of them. When Padre Cornelio came by on his regular visits to 'save' the one Not-Ellerimo would never call Mother, those visits ended inside her so often Not-Ellerimo knew she and her friends called him 'Padre Cornetto', for the size of his member and the things he thought he could do with it. But the Padre would take time now and again to teach him letters—both reading and writing. So la cagna—his head-name for her the first time he learned it, listening at a door while she 'entertained'—would send him, from the age of five, with letters to her 'callers', letters of invitation and of assignation. Those with as little as he and la cagna had would bring meat or fish, gather from the fields, or wood for the fire. Those few with coin would read what he had written, and shake their heads. But still, one evening or many, they would knock at the bitch's door, that very coin in their open hands. And so it was. Five years, six years, seven, eight and nine—and not one birthday for any of them. When he asked her once when he was born, the cuts from the birch twigs lasted for days, weeping puss and blood. He never asked again.

And then it happened.

He was in the woods beyond the glen, for he had loved them from the first time he had escaped there from another of la cagna's rages. Every trail was in his eyes, in his head—in his heart. Not just the trails others knew. But the trails that weren't trails at all, just ways from one place to another, perhaps to run from more birch twigs, or to run and run and runandrun, to runandrunandrunandrunandrun—to feel truly alive and not ever be lost. Deep in the woods he was—and it happened. Because where there had been a rabbit, one he was watching still and silent from behind a bush, not moving a single muscle—suddenly there was no rabbit. Because it swelled and grew, grew and swelled, and it was no rabbit, but a bent over old woman.

And she spat. A spit that flew through the air, flew through the bush he was behind, and landed on his skin. And it burned! Burned like raging fire!

The bent old woman spat again, at the ground this time, ground that sizzled, green carpet crisping and black. "I killed you once. Did she tell you that, marmocchio?" She waited. He didn't move, didn't breathe. "It was today. Auguri per la tua morte, moccio. Today ten years gone. I drank your blood, and took your spirit. I TOOK it! And I left your bitch Moth...."

He leapt from behind the bush. "No Mother of mine, Bruxa!" Because he knew the old tales already, from other children in the village. Knew them, and knew well what they ate. He grabbed a rock from the forest floor, threw it, hard.

The Bruxa cackled. "Yes. I see you have it. Your spirit, marmocchio. AND YOU SHOULD NOT! I ATE YOU!" The bent old woman advanced towards him. And then she was no longer bent, for she towered over him, thrice a woman's tall, one claw-fingered hand reaching over his head—reaching for *him*. "And now I see you here. And that which I ate is whole in you again." The witch sniffs, her nose twitching. "Or near whole. But no matter. Tonight I will feed again. For you are mine! By your Mother's long life and my... no. You are *mine*!"

The loud crack split the grey evening air. The Bruxa's scream? That scream tore that air to shreds. The hand over his head splintered into the night, the hand and fingers torn to their own shreds, and still burning with bright flames. The girl who stepped from shadows, where no shadows had been before she stepped from them, raised an eyebrow, looking at the weapon in her hand. "Barrett M82A1. Damn, Dad's got good taste in guns." She looked up at the Bruxa. "Mind you, he doesn't get all the credit. Making a competition grade round out of cold iron? You gotta admit, I'm an absolute genius." She waved to Not-Ellerimo. "Get behind me, kid." She looked at the Bruxa again. "Haul ass bitch-witch."

The Bruxa screamed—then warped. Shrank. And a rabbit ran from where the girl stood, one foot limping and burning flames even as it healed.

The girl dropped to one knee. "You're tough, kid. But not tough enough, not yet. You've got a road ahead of you, and I can't be there every time. Too dangerous—for both of us. She'll be back. And I won't be there. So remember. Run. I mean, *run*. You know the old oak above your cottage?" He nodded "Run there. It's waiting."

He looked at her. Somehow, this felt familiar—like it had happened before, or would happen some time to come. He knew that didn't make sense—but he knew it did as well. "'It'?"

She smiled. "You're not as dumb as you look. No. Not yet. Everything in its proper time." She stood up. "Hey, sorry. Gotta go. Dad's taking me to the Feast at Hong Gate. We gotta persuade some advisors to disobey their boss. Big pot—time it got stirred up some." The shadows shivered—and the girl was gone. Then the shadows warped again. The girl stepped out. "Damn. I'd forget my head if it was bloody loose. Thiess. Got that? Thiess. It is a name. T, h, i, e, s, s. Thiess. And also, 'Sun and moon go over the sea'. OK? When those words find you? Speak the name." Then the shadows warped, and she was gone.

The woods were deep. And none walked them this late. Which was fortunate. A boy walking through them, muttering to himself, strange magic words of 'this sun and moon, go over the sea' might have found himself on a rack, or a pile of burning kindle. But none were there. None he saw. But deep in the forest, two blood-red eyes opened from sleep.

Chapter 3
Bocca al lupo

FRIULI, ITALY – December 23rd, 1850

Cazzo! The forest streamed past him like a running river, his feet not needing eyes to find their own places to step, push, step-push—to run! Which was good. Because the new-moon sky was dark, though stars pricked the darkness. But he knew well what was behind him had no need of the moon to see him—to find him. To... to.... Merdo! No time. No time to curse fate, curse the one behind him. So he ranandranandran. He needed no trail in these woods, his lungs heaving and gasping, the blood pounding in his head. What he needed was—cazzo! What *was* it? What had she *said*?

He ran.

* * *

FRIULI, ITALY – October, 1847

Being saved by a strange girl from a Bruxa, this was good, yes? Col cavolo. Not for him. He thought about it, as the days passed. Tutto ha un prezzo, yes? That was life, right?

In all his ten years, a slap on the face? That, you could get for free. But nothing good came without a price. Like when Alessio down in the village had told him Alessio's sister would kiss him—but only if he got Alessio a visit with la puttana. Not-Ellerimo, he never got kissed. What he got was a kicking and a beating from Alessio and his friends when he couldn't deliver—and another from la cagna for being foolish enough to ask her. But the girl with the gun? What did *she* want? And each day he wondered. Would it be this one? Today? Tomorrow? But each day passed, and no girl came by with a bill he couldn't pay.

And suns rose. And suns set.

But no girl, and no unknown price to pay, did not mean his days were empty. No Father he knew, and no farm to learn to tend? No importa. Ten years or five, still the work must be done. What work? He learned to repair the cottage, at least, such repairs as did not need gold. And he learned to pick coin from the 'guests' la cagna 'entertained'—a cheeky smile for copper, and a sly hand in a drunkard's temporarily discarded pockets or purses for more while the 'entertainment' was in progress, a more neither the drunkard nor la cagna knew anything of and never saw. But best of all? Most of all? He learned to keep himself and his never-Mother fed. Deep in the woods, he would gather wood for the fire, and meat for the fire also. There was not a rabbit or squirrel safe from his slingshot or the snares he learned to set—and as he grew, sometimes deer and boar would fall to his bow. At ten, he could bring down a boar with one arrow, and a deer with one, perhaps two. But he preferred rabbits. Not for the taste—but cutting and dragging home a boar or deer? That was work and twice work, and that work three times three. His first deer, his arrow went true to the heart. But still, it ran. He had had to chase it, and put a second arrow in to drop it down. He ran to a near farm, excited. Yes, the farmer came. But then he took the deer, all of it, and threw Not-Ellerimo to the ground, laughing. Not-Ellerimo never ran again to any farm. He sought smaller meat, and if he killed larger, then the whole day and much of the night his knife would cut, and his muscles burn as he dragged it back on a branch sled. Today? Today was not a meat day. The previous days had brought rabbits, two squirrels and a chicken, one that must have strayed from some near farm. So meat there was. But meat without a fire? That was wine without grapes. Not that Not-Ellerimo drank wine, unless he stole it in the village, and then la cagna took it from him, mostly. So today? Today he hunted wood.

And deep in the woods—red eyes opened wide.

The woods were dark, even in the day's light, and that light would fail darker before ever he had the wood. He carried his knife, because the woods were not a place to be without one, just as the village was not. And he carried the axe even la cagna had seen he should have, if they were to have wood to burn, to cook—and for her to 'entertain'. A tree? That was beyond his knowing or skill to fall. But branches? Logs? Those he could cut, and then a sled bound with rope, and drag to the cottage. But the trick was not to find wood—just any wood. It had to be wood that would burn now. Not wet or green, not dry and crumbled. Solid logs sufficiently dry or pine-sapped to burn warm and bright. But not so big he could not get it to the cottage. He knew the trails, the places wood fell—but still it was like the men in the village Mescita, jugs close to their hands as the dice rolled for who would pay. Wood was where it was—not always or even often where it had been. So he was deep in the woods when it happened.

An arm snaked round him from behind, a knife sharp at his throat. "Sun and moon, brat. Sun and moon go over the sea. Tell me my name?" Not-Ellerimo gasped, the gasp itself drawing blood from the blade across his throat. But the words? Those words he knew. Was it now? What...? He gasped again as the blade slid tighter on him. "What's my name brat?"

Not-Ellerimo stilled. He drew breath gently. Held it—and gently let it out. If the knife had wanted him dead, then dead he would be. So... "Thiess. She—she said your name was Thiess."

The knife pulled away from his throat. Hands spun him round, pushed him flat-back to the ground. The man was old, but muscles still showed over bone-stretched skin. The old man raised one eyebrow. "Thiess of Kaltenbrun, were we in polite company. But since neither of us is, polite company I mean, Thiess will do. Though if you ever speak that name to another I'll kill you, and the Shadow Child can do as she will."

"Shadow Child?"

"No matter, brat. That—that is another tale, for another day." The old man shook his head. "And I'm still not sure I believe which 'other day' that means. Who she is? Well, ükskõik millal sa soovid. But I owe her, and she *always* collects her debts, that one. And now you are mine. My debt. I'm told you have witch problems." The man spat. "Pfah—nõiduma. Witches. May they burn, and me the one to set the match." He paused. "Though not all are black, this you must know." The old man looked at Not-Ellerimo. Shaking his head. He spat again. "Pfah. You know nothing, do you boy?" Not-Ellerimo wondered how he had graduated from 'brat' to 'boy'. "Well, no matter. A debt is a debt. Soon you will know more, though perhaps you will regret the knowing. What do you seek? I've seen you pass the rabbit holes and such."

Not-Ellerimo struggled to his feet. "I seek wood sir. For—for my..." he bit his lip, his eyes, he knew, growing cold. "For my Mother's fi..."

The old man spat again. "She's no Mother of yours boy. And if she ever was, she ceased being so the night you first died. So spit on her name, as I do, and let her fate be no better than she deserves. But not yet. No. For now? For now, we find wood." As the old man spoke, Not-Ellerimo's cold eyes saw them. Two old eyes—burning blood red in the greying light.

* * *

FRIULI, ITALY – December 23rd, 1850

His feet thudded on the grassy ground. Behind him, brush crackled, trees creaked. He ran, lungs heaving, his mind filled with red eyes, with the blood, with the howling.

He ran.

* * *

FRIULI, ITALY – November, 1848

"No boy. She's not a witch, your... I mean, la cagna. No. She just knows some things—some ways to call one. A Bruxa. La puttana? Her trade? I have nothing against it. But, kõigel on oma hind, you know? And her way of paying her profession's price? She could go to the ruota degli esposti, and none would care. But no. She calls. She calls, and the Bruxa comes. Comes—and eats. What

41

does la cagna get? I know not and care less. Perhaps you do, and perhaps there are things you *will* do. But I care not about those either. My debt is you."

"Me?"

"Yes boy. You. You died. But she needs you alive. So..."

"I *died*?"

Thiess sighed. "I'm too old for this. I mean, *really* too old. Two hundred and thirty years I have walked these lands, and..."

"Liar!"

The old man raised an eyebrow. "I told her I would never hit you. But I cannot say I have always kept all of my promises. I will not lie to you, young cub. Come with me."

The woods were dark. Not-Ellerimo was hunting—or at least, that was what he had told la cagna. Told her every day and every night he came to the woods. And truly, he returned with meat, with wood—as much as was needed, and even some to sell. But not because he caught it alone. Thiess had already taught him much. They walked to a clearing. Thiess began to shed his clothes. Not-Ellerimo covered his eyes. "What...?"

"Uncover your eyes, young cub. You must see this."

"I..."

"Uncover. Your. Eyes."

Not-Ellerimo uncovered his eyes. And watched, as bones and muscles flowed and stretched—as skin became fur. And listened to the howl that split the night. Then bones and muscles stretched and flowed again—fur became skin. The old man stood. "Truly, I am not as young as once I was. That—well, it hurts. So. You understand?"

"Lupo! lupo mannaro!" Not-Ellerimo made the sign of the cross over his chest. "Dio mi salvi!" He raised his knife.

"Oh, please. Do stop that. Do you see me bursting into flames? Do you see God's fire burning me?"

"But... but..."

"What you call them. Werewolves. Evil demons, who take a man—tell me, why is it always a man? Porcheria. It is like witches. Always, always women. Merda, it is not so. Men are witches, women are—pfah!" The old man shook his head. "Kontrolli end, Thiess. Kontrolli!" He shook his head again. "No matter. What is it you say? Non importa, that is it. Yes, I am over two hundred years old. Yes, I am sometimes a wolf. But demon? No! Not ever! Those like me? We were of God! Hounds of God! We hunted the nõiduma, went down to Inferno, to Hell, and took the grain and livestock they stole, the fruits— and brought them back! So the harvest would be... ah, mida perset. No matter. That was long ago, and my country is gone. But you had us here too. The Benandanti. You know them? The ones who fought the witches, with their wolf friends? The Good Walkers? Dio mio, what is the matter with today. History is—oh, no matter. Look. It is like this. You were born. Your Mo... the one who brought you forth called a witch. She ate you, your blood, your spirit. But then? Then you were born. Because *she* came. And now you owe her. But not yet. Not. Yet. Because first?"

"First?"

"First, you have to bloody KILL the bitch who killed you!"

Chapter 4

Vivere al lupo

FRIULI, ITALY – December 23rd, 1850

Cazzo! What *was* it? What had she *said*?

He ran.

She said... she said... that's it! The oak! He turned, twisted the path his feet were making. The cottage was not near. The sounds behind him? Were.

He ran.

* * *

FRIULI, ITALY – January, 1848

"Can I be a wolf?"

"You, young cub? Can I pass my gift, my curse, my duty and my honour to you? I am old. Tired. My people are gone, the Benandanti here are gone from here—the good witches, those who protected the land. Good Walkers, they were. Pfah. Do you know how long I have looked for someone to even *ask*? Shall I tell you a story, young cub? How I became a Hound of God? I was bloody tricked! I was a beggar. A nothing and a nobody. One day, I am begging my day's bread, and a man comes to me. He says he will give me gold, and buy me beer! Well, what is a one like me to do? I go with him. He buys two beers. Well, that is what I *thought* he did. Värdjas! He drank, I drank. Värdjas! He laughed at me! Told me I was now a Hound, and he was free! Then they came for me, my new people. They told me about the witches, about Hell. Two hundred bloody years I have looked for someone to buy a drink for! I put salt blessed by a holy man into the beer, and toast them. I breathe into the jug three times and say "you will become like me." I am old. I am tired. But in two hundred years? I have found nobody to chase the witches. And now? Even your witch? When I was young, I could have torn her limb from limb. But—I am old. And useless. For my muscles, anyway. But for what I know? This is not useless. Now. To fell a tree, it is not easy. There are cuts to make, and places most definitely not to stand. Watch me..."

* * *

FRIULI, ITALY – February, 1848
"Close your eyes."
"What? Why... what?"
"I said, close your eyes. Now. Walk with me."

To say it was far? What is that? Tired feet, yes. No sense of where the path had led? Twice yes. Trees bent heavy overhead, but

46

trees Not-Ellerimo had ever known? Yes, and yes and yes once more. And three times was old as old, this Not-Ellerimo knew. "Where are we?"

"Does it matter?"

"I... where is... are we lost?"

"No."

"Then where...?"

"*We* are not lost. For I know my way to any place you would have us travel, and would had it been you bringing me here with my eyes closed tight. Are *you* lost?"

"I... yes. I am lost." Not-Ellerimo reached into his pack, and pulled from it a lodestone, set in wood, that he had taken from one of la cagna's 'guests' while that guest was being 'entertained'. "No matter. I will..."

Thiess' hand was swift. The claws springing from it were sharp. The lodestone's case shattered. "And now? Pfah. Are you a two-leg or a four? Tell me, when did you ever see a wolf lost, or lost and gazing at a nonsense scrap of iron that it might find its path? You do not need such luxuries. If I ever see one in your paw again, truly I will set your blood to water the grasses." Thiess waved his arm. "There is sun, even if the trees hide it. There is moon, were it night. There is wind and ear, smell and sound. Find your path home young almost-wolf. Even on two legs, we are not as others are. Come. Let me teach you." Thiess sighed. "Truly, I am too old for this. But no matter. Crouch down. See this tree? Now..."

* * *

FRIULI, ITALY – March, 1848
"I do not believe you."

"I have told you once, young cub. I will not lie to you. Call me liar again and whatever the Shadow Child wishes, I will kill you myself. Yes, I went to Hell. Many times. Three times each year."

"How?"

"Oh, young cub. Going to Hell? It is easy. There are places, if you know where to find them. In my day, we went to a place beyond the sea, a swamp near Lemburg. When you go to such a place, there is a path. And it is easy! You cut your finger, and mix it with— well, with your juice that makes babies. Yes, women can do that too. You will learn as you grow. But you mix it, then rub it across your eyes, and you will see the path. You walk that path, walk and walk—and that is it. You will find Hell. And if you are foolish enough to have done it? Well, you will never return. For a live body, human, wolf or witch? There is no escape, servant of the Devil or of God. The path is locked."

"Hah! But you are here, so *you* escaped! Many times, you say!"

"Yes I did, young cub. I and my people, when we went to fight the Devil and the witches? Hah! Some of us would turn to

48

human, and some of us to wolf. The humans would strike the witches with cold iron rods, for they are weak to cold iron…"

"Like her bullet!"

"Yes. Like her bullet. And the wolves of us would chase them and rend them! We would take what they had stolen and return it to the human world, to secure the harvest!"

"So you killed them?"

"No. We could not. Because to return, we must not be there. So when we went to the marsh, we would cut ourselves and mix the blood with our essence. And we would wipe it over our eyes—then sleep. Because then only our spirits would go. And a spirit can return. But a spirit cannot kill in Hell, as the witches were spirits also."

"Are there places here?"

"What? Places? To Hell? How would I know? I am from Livonia! The Benandanti would perhaps have known, but they are gone. Now. You swing an axe like a butterfly swinging a pig. Watch me. Like this…"

* * *

FRIULI, ITALY – December 23rd, 1850

The lights burned in the cottage. Clearly, la cagna was working her trade. He could see it. The oak!

He ran.

* * *

FRIULI, ITALY – June, 1849

"Will you come with me? I have a thing for you."

"A thing? What thing, young cub?"

"It is—it is just a thing."

"I see your plan. You are trying to get out of your lessons again! Well, if you can tell me how to…"

"Will you come with me?" Not-Ellerimo stood from the mushrooms they were examining. He walked, hearing the old man behind him. In the clearing, they were there, where he had left them. The two mugs. He didn't turn, just spoke to the air. "Padre Cornelio thought I was crazy. Or a sinner. Of course, he thinks everyone is a sinner, apart from him. But I told him I would tell la cagna he had the sinner disease, the one you get from sin. She would never 'entertain' him again. So he blessed it." Not-Ellerimo pulled the bag of salt from his pocket. "I think I am old enough. For a beer, I mean. We should…" he turned to face the old man "… we should have a toast, don't you think?"

The old man's eyes burned with red fire, and tears also. "You mean…?"

Not-Ellerimo shrugged. "You said in your youth, you could have rended her. Me? I am young."

"But—but—the Shadow Chi…"

Not-Ellerimo put one hand on the old man's mouth. "Did she say not to?"

50

"She did not know my tale."

"Are you sure?"

"I..."

"Sit, sir. Please sit? Please?"

They sat. The old man put salt into both beers. He whispered over them. "You will become like me." He took his beer, handed Not-Ellerimo his. They drank.

Not-Ellerimo shrugged. "Now what? I feel no different?"

The old man slumped. Bones and muscles flowed and stretched—as skin became fur. And a howl fit to split the sky came from wolf lips. Then bones and muscles stretched and flowed again—fur became skin. The old man stood, blood tears falling from blood-red eyes. And another, all too human howl split the skies.

* * *

FRIULI, ITALY – December 23rd, 1850

"I am done."

Not-Ellerimo looked at the old man. "Done?"

"It is tonight. Ember night. She will come. She will come, and I have tried. Tried to teach you. And you have learned well. But..."

"But you are old, and I—I am not a wolf."

"I will fight her. Fight her with all I have. But..."

"But as the child said, old man. You are old." The rabbit that had bounded from the trees was a rabbit no more. The Bruxa stood, and cackled her laugh. "And he is no young wolf, to make me fear and call my sisters. I will eat him this night, and none shall stop me!"

"Yes, witch. I am old. And I am not what I was." Thiess stood. "But I am still what I am. Run, young cub! Run!"

* * *

FRIULI, ITALY – December 23rd, 1850

He ran. Behind him, the battle spoke loud. He ran. And ran and ran—until one last dying howl split the night. One last howl and, he knew, red tears falling from dimming red eyes.

He ran.

* * *

FRIULI, ITALY – December 23rd, 1850

He ran. The oak was near. But—but what was that? There, in the grass? A laughing cackle came from behind, and a clawed hand grasped his ankle. He fell, his hand closing on the glint in the grass.

52

"You are mine now, brat! When she woke you, I felt the hole tear in my spirit. Now I will fill that hole."

He rolled over, staring the Bruxa in the face. "Perhaps, witch. But—perhaps not! Pfah!" He spat in her face—and pulled the dagger with strange marking from behind him. He stabbed it, deep in her heart.

"No! Not..." The witch screamed. Then she stopped. She looked down. "What?" No blood seeped from the dagger, though a wound closed behind it as it fell to the ground. The Bruxa laughed. "I don't know what you thought you had made, brat. But whatever it was? It matters not." She picked him up, and with one hand, snapped each leg at the knee. "Now you are mine. But I think— yes. I think your toy will serve to give me my rightful drink." She laughed again—and plunged the dagger into his own heart. And then gasped as the third quarter moon above turned blood red. "No! No! I..."

From the oak tree bark, the wolf skin dropped to his back, sank into his flesh. He felt his legs twist and mend, bones and muscles flow and stretch—as skin became fur. A howl fit to split the sky came from wolf lips. And a wolf leapt from the ground and tore at the Bruxa, as she pulled on the dagger buried in its flesh. A dagger that would not pull free. And the Hound's claws tore at her flesh. Tore and tore—tore and tore. Then the Hound ran, tattered rags on the ground behind him. Ran and ran and ran and

ranandranandran—deep into the woods, as
witch screams echoed behind him.

Chapter 5

Benandanti

FRIULI, ITALY – December 24th, 1850

A forest clearing. And a beast sat in the clearing, licking bloody claws. The dagger still deep in its flesh twitched as it breathed. One claw reached for the dagger—pulled. The dagger slid free, and a naked Not-Ellerimo stood in the clearing, wounds healed, though scars remained. He looked up at the white moon. He flexed muscles—focused his thoughts. He looked down at a very not-wolf body. He raised an eyebrow—and turned for the cottage.

* * *

Not-Ellerimo pushed the door wide. She was there, still but part-clothed from her 'entertainment'. He looked down. Not, of course, that he could talk. He looked at her. "Greetings, cagna."

"Bastardo!" Old, wrinkled hands clawed at a face no 'guest' would wish to 'entertain' them. "Bastardo!". His not-Mother turned, the same clawed hands lashing out. "Bast...".

He caught both hands, mid-lash. His fingers closed on them, and faint cracks came from the bones in her wrists. "I see. He was right. You do get your rewards for what you feed her."

"He? What he? Bastardo! I will..."

"You will what, bitch?" He threw her hands down. "You will go to Padre Cornetto and tell him your evil son has near killed the witch you serve?"

"*Near* killed? Wha..."

"Shut up."

"You cannot talk to me like that! I am your Mo..."

His hand lashed out. The slap was loud. "Never. Never use that word to me, cagna. Sadly, I do not think your witch is dead. I think I would know it. So perhaps your, what? Your 'goods in trade'? Perhaps they will return. I do not care. You do what you wish. But if you say one word of me? Then—well. 'Then'."

"Bastardo! Bast... *Bastardo!*" A clawed hand stretched, reached for the eldritch blade in his belt. "*BASTARDO!*" She plunged the blade into him. And the flesh round the blade flowed. Flesh flowed, and bones twisted. The Hound growled, softly. Then bones twisted—flesh flowed again. And red eyes colder than ice smiled, as a howl rent the night air.

La cagna screamed. "Lupo! Lupo mann..."

"No." The woman at the door was old, one eye covered by a patch. "Not at all, Bruxa-schiava. No, the weres you speak of? They serve the devil." The old woman smiled at the Hound. "Soft, youngling. Soft." Hound claws reached, pulled. The dagger slid free. Muscles and bones flowed, twisted—and the old woman raised one eyebrow at the naked Not-Ellerimo. "Hmmm. I see. Or rather—I do not. Do you know how unusual that is for me, youngling? Well." The old woman looked at la cagna. "No. He is a Hound of God." The old woman looked at Not-Ellerimo. "Or perhaps not—he is, a puzzlement." She turned. "But you, cagna? You are no puzzle at all." The old woman's fingers danced in the air. As they danced, the air began to sizzle.

La cagna blanched. "Benandanti! Ben... but you are all gone! You are dead! My mistress, she tol..."

The old woman smiled, but it was cold. "She told you? She told you of the Battle? How we went to the Hells, and we were wiped from the Earth? Well, she did not quite lie. Most of us? Yes. Morto. All of us? Not ever." The old woman looked at Not-Ellerimo. "You know she is not dead, yes? The Bruxa?"

Not-Ellerimo shrugged. "Yes."

"And what will you do?"

He shrugged again. "I will live here. I will wait. And she will come. And maybe she will

57

die, and maybe I will die. But it will be as it must.”

The old woman raised an eyebrow. “Perhaps. But which would you prefer?”

“My living has not been so sweet. Until...”

“Until...?” The old woman smiled. “Ah, yes. ‘Sun and moon go over the sea.’ He was a brave man, Thiess. One of our best.”

“You knew Thiess?” Not-Ellerimo stepped forward. “How...?”

The old woman smiled. “Three hundred years and more I have walked these lands, youngling. I have known many.” She smiled again. “You may call me Caterina.” Her fingers lifted, touched the patch on her eye. “Caterina la Guercia, so they called me when the world first thought I was old.” She looked round the cottage. “Yes. This will do. For now—not forever. A long road waits for you youngling. A long road and a distant land. But first? First you have much to learn.”

“Thiess taught me much...” Not-Ellerimo paused... “... wise one.”

The old woman laughed. “Yes, he did. But I do not seek to teach you to chop trees youngling. Or to run the night winds to their exhaustion, or to fight with tooth and claw. No. My teaching? There are witches, young Benandanti. And to fight a witch? Blade is not enough. Tooth is not enough, nor claw. To fight a witch? Then a witch you must be also. Vedi?”

He looked at the old woman. Looked at la cagna. "If I must, I would rather be you than..." He spat. "... than her."

The old woman smiled. "Worthy spoken youngling." She looked at la cagna. "Though the words are dust in my mouth, I will help you. Your mistress's powers are weak." She smiled at Not-Ellerimo. "The youngling mauled your mistress deep and sore. But it is better if things remain, to the passing eye, as they are. He will stay here, and come to me for teaching. You will stay here and..." The old woman's fingers danced, and the years fell from la cagna "... and ply your 'trade'. But if you say one word? Then I will take back my gift before he raises a claw, and he will kill you—but you will die old and die ugly, bitch. Do you understand?"

"Ye... yes. I understand." The look la cagna cast at both of them would have burned ice to fire—but neither Not-Ellerimo. or the old woman so much as flinched. "Yes."

The old woman nodded her head. "So let it be." She turned to Not-Ellerimo. "The glade where you met him. Tomorrow. Tomorrow and every tomorrow I speak—be there." She waited, until Not-Ellerimo. nodded. "Bene. Let it be so. Oh, and youngling?"

"Yes, old one?"

The old woman grinned. "Put on some clothes." And she was gone.

***

FRIULI, ITALY – January, 1851
"I lied to your M... to her."

Not-Ellerimo waited.

The old woman raised an eyebrow. "You listen when most would speak. You are not as foolish as I thought you might be. Did Thiess teach you that?"

He waited, then raised one eyebrow, a half smile on his lips.

"I see." She smiled also. "Well. I lied. Or I did not. Or I did not, but it will become a lie. One of those—or perhaps all of them. You see, I cannot teach you to become a witch, of any kind—black, white, blue, green or purple? Pfah. There are no colours to what those who know nothing call witches. It is what they do with what they are. Because a witch? A witch does not learn to have power. They have power from their very nature. They may be taught how to control it, how to use it. But first? First, they must have it. Like you."

"Like me?"

"Like you—but not like you. Or both. You? You puzzle me, youngling. You have no power. I can sense this. But you *must* have power, or you could not be Hound. But it is not part of you. *She* put it in you, but I know not how. It is—una perplessità."

She. The girl. The—what had Thiess called her? The Shadow Child. He nodded. "I apologise, wise one."

"Oh, no apologies needed youngling. I am old. Indovinelli are all I have left. But…"

"No, wise one. I apologise. It is—no matter." He stood, took off his clothes. The old woman raised an eyebrow, but waited. He took the dagger—and plunged it into his chest. Muscles flowed, bones twisted. One clawed foot raised, and pulled the dagger from a chest that did not bleed, a wound that sealed. Not-Ellerimo gasped, but put on his clothes. He looked at the old woman. He shrugged, one eyebrow raised.

The old woman nodded slowly. "Yes. I see. Why she chose you—why she made you. Or maybe I do not. Why? Why is a blade of many edges. But—yes. Does it hurt?"

"Hurt? As a million coals on my skin." He shrugged again, a lip ruefully twisted.

"May I see it?"

"No." The girl stepped from the trees. "Do you know how long it took Waylan to carve those eldritch runes? And I don't even know what bloody eldritch *is*. I had to get bloody Hauras to tell me how to find Waylan, and…"

The old woman blanched. "Hauras? You consort with *demons*? Then you must die!" The old woman's fingers danced, air sizzling.

The girl sighed. "Even *I'm* too old for this." She took a chalk from her pocket, reached down and drew a triangle, with strange symbols. "Haura…"

The man-leopard in the triangle sighed. "Ow! My head *hurts*! You're worse than your damned" —the man-leopard looked up—"er, I mean, you're worse than your bloody Father girl!" The man-leopard looked at the old woman. "You know who I am, yes?"

"Yes! But..."

"Look, you know who I am, and you see I'm in a bloody triangle, and you know what that means, yes?"

"Yes, yes! But..."

The man-leopard sighed, braced his shoulders. "OK. Here goes. Bymynameandmywordthegirlisnotevilandc anbetrusted." The man-demon grabbed his head. "I bloody swear. This girl? Her Father? *I'm* too old for this." He looked at the girl. "Are we done here?"

The girl grinned. "Depends. What would you say about next week's lottery numbers?" She laughs. "Yes, we're done. Scat, kitty-cat."

"Kitty-cat? *Kitty*-ca...?" The triangle sits empty.

"Knife." The girl held out her hand. Not-Ellerimo gave it to her. She waved her hand over it, muttered words. The blade hilt folded open. Inside was a soggy mass, bright red. The girl prodded it. "Alginate-based hydrogel. I swear, this stuff sucks better than a New York hooke..." She looked up. "Ahem. Never mind. Look. Thiess couldn't pass his power to you. You are... no matter. You needed the blade and skin. This? It is... it is no matter. But it has power. Let us say, a gift. I say again—*it* has power. You..." She nodded at Not-Ellerimo "... don't. Each time you

62

turn? Some blood gets used up. It will be less. So no stabbing yourself just to impress girls, OK? Here." She handed the knife to Not-Ellerimo. "But you shouldn't show it in plain sight. So I took care of that. Watch." The girl took the knife, put it to Not-Ellerimo's thigh. The skin split–opened, and the knife, though far too large, slid inside, and was gone. The girl winked at Not-Ellerimo. "Pocket universe. My not-Mom had a thing for them. Like my Glock." At Not-Ellerimo's confused look, she shook her head. "Never mind. Now. When you need it? Your blade? Put your hand on your leg." When Not-Ellerimo placed his hand where she pointed? His skin and flesh split, with no trace of blood, and his knife was bare in his grip. The girl nodded. "Yeah. Like that." She turned—and was gone.

The old woman looked at the dagger. She looked at Not-Ellerimo. She looked at the triangle on the floor, then hastily rubbed it out with her foot. "I, ah, I see. Or I do not. One of those. But, well... but. Apparently you are not a witch. You have power. But it is not yours, only borrowed. And not forever, do you see? Each time you use it, it is less. Some day? Some day it will be gone. Unless... pfah. No matter. But for now? For now you can be a Hound. But later? Later will come too. And for then? For then you must be a sorcerer."

"A sorcerer?"

"Yes. Sorcerers, they also do not have power. But they have learned to control the powers around them. It is like—like, when you are Hound, you can run, yes?"

"Yes! I run and run! I runandrunandrunand..."

The old woman chuckled. "Yes, I see you do. But you run, so far, so swift, because of what you are. A sorcerer, man or woman? They cannot run. But they are like a man who has a horse. They can make the horse move them swiftly, and maybe? Maybe even swift enough to catch a Hound, yes?"

"I... I see. I think?"

"So if one day you must catch a witch? And are no Hound to run the wind to exhaustion? Then? Then you must be a sorcerer. One who needs not be a Hound."

"Capisco." He pursed his lips. "So how do I learn?"

She laughed. "Mostly? Mostly, you listen. This you do well, I see. But also?"

"Also?"

"Well, I am an old woman. A little old to hunt. And I do love wild pig..." The old woman laughed again. After a moment, so did he. "I will get my bow, wise one."

* * *

"So. You are in the village. No, in a strange village. And you wish to find la cagna, for you know she is there somewhere. How?"

"Cazzo. She can die in her own vomit there if she chooses. I would not seek…"

The slap on his cheek was light—but firm. "Pay attention youngling! What I teach, few can offer! Perhaps she stole your gold. Perhaps she must die, and yours the blade to do it. I do not care! How do you find her?"

He shrugged. Rubbing his cheek. "I ask people. I describe her. I…"

"So you wander the village, and you—you what? You ask random strangers for what you seek?" The slap was harder. Firmer.

"No! No. I—I seek the places she would seek. *Then* I describe. *Then* I ask."

"Thus and so. So you know her spirit, so you seek where her spirit would seek, yes?"

"I suppose. If that is how you put it."

"It is not how I put it. It is how it is. People? People do not change, not at their core. And for a sorcerer? It is the same. You must have their core, their spirit, or some part of it, to find them. It is said, that which is once together, is never parted. And so, and listen well, get you a lodestone—the iron or the rock that ever seeks North. Get you a piece of that you seek. A hair, a sneezed rag, a soiled undergarment—blood soiled or nightsoiled. Take a small piece of thread and wrap it to the lodestone. Put it in oil, that it floats, in a vessel, and let it sit in the moon's light for three nights..."

"I see. So if I ever wish to find la cagna, I can..."

This time the slap was hard. Very hard. "No, youngling. No. Do you not see? Tell me, when the Bruxa stabbed you, did you rend her?"

"Yes! Yes, I Shifted, and I clawed her, and..."

"Yes, yes. I am sure you did. But did *she* rend *you*?"

"She had claws. Yes, but I clawed *her*, and then I ra..."

The hardest slap. Twice. "And did you bleed, foolish youngling? Did her claws carry your blood, and the grass the same? And did she, perhaps, come back after you were gone, and gather that blood? And might she, perhaps, know at least as much of sorcery as I, she who has lived as many years as I have breathed breaths? And might she know..."

Not-Ellerimo nodded. "I see. Know how to craft a lodestone, with my blood, and follow its voice to find me?" He nods again, sits. He waits.

The old woman nodded. She looked up at the girl in the shadows, the one she knew Not-Ellerimo. could not see—the girl with sad eyes. The girl nodded—and was gone.

Chapter 6

Stregoni

FRIULI, ITALY – December, 1853
The grey evening wind was cold, and strong. The noose swung in it, the body heavy beneath it. She took something from her pack, a withered hand, and set a wick to one of the fingers. She lit the wick—and the few people near the gibbet froze still. The old woman nodded at Not-Ellerimo. "You know what you must do."

He sighed, and reached for the cold-iron dagger in his belt, fresh made the previous night under a bright moon. He walked up the gallows steps, and took the corpse's hand. The cold iron cut through flesh, through bone. He wrapped it in cloth he took from his pack, then took another cut hand from the same pack. He plucked hairs from the corpse's head, and threaded them to a cold iron needle, fresh made under the same moon the previous night. Then he sewed the second hand on to the bare wrist. A glance at the moon, a wave of hand, and some words— and the hand looked as though it sat a wrist it was born to. The cold iron blade sliced into the corpse's fat belly, and cut, sliced and

67

cut—and Not-Ellerimo took the fat from the belly, and wrapped it also in cloth. The needle, more hair from the corpse's head—and no sign of cut or injury remained. He walked down the steps. The old woman blew out the wick of the corpse-candle she carried, and the few passers-by passed their way by. The old woman nodded. "And what next?"

Not-Ellerimo sighed. "Why do I need this?"

The old woman raised an eyebrow, "Perhaps you do not. Throw it away then."

Not-Ellerimo sighed. Again. "And if I do and if ever I have need of such a thing?"

The old woman shrugged. "Perhaps you will need it, not know how to have it—and die. Or perhaps not. But tell me. If you wish to avoid being hunted by an eagle, do you study fish?"

Not-Ellerimo sighed. He was getting used to it. "So?"

"So. What next?"

"Next? Salt, pisciare of man, of woman, of sheep, of cat and horse. Oh, of horse and mare both. And... and the rest. Must I? You know I know it."

"Very well. Show me." The two turned—and were gone.

* * *

FRIULI, ITALY – April, 1854
The two Candles set in the two hands burned gently in the night. "So." The old

woman pointed at the Candles. "If a Candle burns, and all those near are frozen still, why am I not frozen?"

Not-Ellerimo shrugged. "Because while, yes, my Candle burns, so does yours. And yours burns next to it. If your Candle was not burning, would you also be frozen?"

"A good question, youngling. And the answer is no. And yes also. No, because I am a witch, and the Candle has no power over me, but if I were not? Then yes. If my Candle was not burning, I would be frozen still, and if my Candle was burning, but not in sight of yours, then the same. Also, if you carry a corpse-candle, and you touch another, then? Then the Candle's power will not hold them, vedi? So. Is that why I had you make this, do you think?"

Not-Ellerimo stayed silent, one eyebrow raised.

The old woman nodded, smiled. "I see. No, it is not. Take your Candle and come with me." He took his candle in his dead hand. They walked to the cottage. The old woman entered, and he heard the door bar being set. She nodded at him, motioned her hand. Face set tight, he held his candle-hand up—and walked. Walked and walked—and walked through the door.

"Do you see? The world's barriers? They set no bar to one with a Candle. But be wary. For if your Candle snuffs its flame? Or if the wax burns too low and is no more? Then the world's way returns. Not in any instant, but if you do not pay heed? Then you will be frozen also—mayhap part in, part out, and that freezing never to pass.”

* * *

FRIULI, ITALY – May, 1854
“Wake up youngling.”

“Whuh… old one, what is wrong?” His hand went to the cold iron blade ever on his belt.

“Wrong? Nothing. Oh—you should most like stop the bleeding, no?”

“Bleeding?”

She held it up in front of him—a flap of thinnest skin. She pointed to his shoulder. “I took it from there. As you slept, and never felt a thing. Then I stuck you, to wake you.”

“You stabbed me?”

“Yes. To wake you.” She held it up before his eyes. A small edge, set to a wood haft. “Fire glass it is, taken from the burning mountains. It has an edge sharper than any steel.”

He took it from her, examining it closely. He looked up, one eyebrow raised, but his tongue silent.

She nodded. “Indeed. To hear, one must first be silent, yes? Brittle it is, for it is glass. But so very, very sharp. A flap of skin—not meat, but skin—and the one it is taken from still sleeping.”

“Skin. For?”

70

"Ah, indeed. For what, sì? Well, for, mayhap, a binding or a finding. Once together, always together, yes? Or to cover a scar, or ink, that might give away one who wishes to stay hidden?"

"But to cover? What may hold it to that covered?"

"Indeed. The root of comfrey, root of lobelia—some of each, ground fine of fine. honey from a hive, the core of wheat seed pressed for its blood, and pressed three times. Once under noon sun, once under midnight moon and once in the wolf light as night passes to day. Truly, it will glue skin to flesh, and no sign of stitch! For smaller needs, at least. For larger wounds? As at the gallows. Cold iron needle, never used before and never after that one flesh, and most private hair, from those parts others do not see to sew it. Soak the hair in fresh fallen rain and fresh ground salt, mix in first-dew spider-web and grey aged, ground up pine needles. It will hold and hold, and never be seen. Oh. And truly—stanch the blood, youngling. Never let a drop of yours fall where some other may gather it, yes?"

* * *

FRIULI, ITALY – June, 1854

"Pfah! May the Powers weep, youngling! There is so little time, and so much I must tell you, so much I *could* tell! Why, herb-lore alone! Yes, yes. For the most part, folk seek women. Can men not heal also? Why, of course! Al-Zahrawi, for I have spoken oft with his spirit. Old Galen, aye—so many. To stanch a wound? Yes. To set a maid's moon aright after some foolish dalliance? Yes. To give strength, to cure a poison? Yes. That poison itself? Yes, yes and thrice yes! So much. Take your book youngling and let us walk. There are things to gather, and more to craft!"

* * *

FRIULI, ITALY – July, 1854
"Thus and so. So a Dead-Hand-Candle will let you through any door, yes?"

"Apparently."

"Apparently?"

"Well, yes, to those you have shown me. But?"

The old woman raised an eyebrow. "But?"

He smiled. "But your lessons almost never have one page to their book wise one."

She smiled also. "You grow swiftly. But yes. As with fire, there is ice."

"And as with this fire, what if my enemy has it, and I sit behind barred doors that are no bar? Is this your page I must scry today wise one?"

The old woman laughed. "Well and well, well and better youngling. Thus. To bar your door from Candles, this you must do. To the door frames, the windows, any place of entry. When the Dog Star rises near the sun, the dies canulares at the end of Summer, then mix the gall of a black cat, the fat of a red rooster, and the tears of a swan. Then set this unguent to the places of entry, and none may enter by power of the dead hand."

"I see. And how does one make a swan to cry wise one?"

She looked at him sharply, but he was grinning. She smiled also. "Perhaps by giving it a pupil as knot-minded as you, youngling. That, shall we say, is a lesson for the student. Now. On the summoning of the elements."

They looked up, the noise of the rain pounding on the cottage roof. "Ahem. I was going to start with fire, but I see the Powers perhaps have a sense of humour. So, no matter. To summon water..."

* * *

FRIULI, ITALY – November 10th, 1854
"It comes. The Ember tide. And Saint Lucia's fest with it."

He looked up from the book he had written of her words. "I know."

The old woman looked sad. "Once—once there were so many of us. And the Ember days would come, and we would travel. Did Thiess tell you of this?

Not-Ellerimo nodded. "Inferno? Certo. The iron bars. The broom shafts and the horses tails? Aye. But—where did he say, Lemburg? I know not this place."

"Still and all. It comes. And we must travel."

"To Lemburg?"

"No. To another place. One you must find, for it must be one your heart and spirit recognise."

"We travel? To slay her? Down deep, in the black place?"

"No. Not slay. She is there in spirit only, so there she cannot die. And not even to find her, not yet. So you must know the path, the passage to Inferno."

"Why? If I cannot kill her there, then...?"

The old woman smiled. But that smile was grim. "Un enigma, sì? But that is not for now. Now? Now is to know the path. Yes, that. Yes, one day you must kill her, or she will kill you. And that day will come, though it will not find you in this land. And the Shadow Child apart? Well. Who does not wish to live, sì?"

He tilted his head. "My life has not always been one I wished to live, old Mother." He pretended not to see the faint blush on old cheeks. "But first Thiess? And then..." he felt his own cheeks blush "... well, and then? Perhaps I could wish more years."

She smiled. "Thus and so. Youngling I have called you, but perhaps fledgling would be better marked. And now? The nest cannot be your home forever. You must fly, wolf walker."

He grinned. "A flying wolf? Now that would be a thing indeed."

The slap was loud—but gentle. "Prestare attenzione, young wolf. Or rather, stregoni. For if you were wolf? As Thiess was wolf? You would know this, from your spirit and its nature. But you do not. And I cannot tell you. Is there a place? Yes. There is always a place. But *your* place? For it to be yours, *you* must find it. Think on what you know, what Thiess told you. And then hunt. But hunt as a wolf hunts, not as a sorcerer would hunt. Your place does not lie in old tales, or torn books. It lies—it lies where you must find it."

He nodded. Nodded and sighed and took off his clothes. Then his hand reached for his thigh, and the dagger he carried in a place that could not exist was in his hand. "As you say old Mother. As you say. Vado a caccia." A blade carved with eldritch symbols plunged into a young chest, a howl ripping the night air—and a wolf ran from the cottage door.

* * *

FRIULI, ITALY – November 20th, 1854

The wolf padded in through the cottage door. A clawed pad grasped the dagger tight-buried in its flesh—grasped and pulled. Muscles flowed, bones twisted—and the wolf was gone. "*Vaffanculo! Merda,* that hurts!"

The old woman looked up. "A dagger in the chest? Questo non è niente. You should try being burned." She looked up, her head tilted and eyes distant. "Three times. Or was it four? No matter. How went your hunt, youngling?"

Not-Ellerimo set the dagger back to his thigh, and it was gone. "Isola della Conna. The swamp that is a river. Or, perhaps the river that is a swamp. It spoke to me. Swamp or river, it is my road."

The old woman nodded, slowly. "Ah, indeed. The Road that is a river. That is…" she looked up. "No matter. If your hunt found it, then it is yours, your Truth." She nodded again. "And mine also, for while I will guide you, you must take me."

He raised one eyebrow, his mouth silent.

She smiled, shook her head. "I am glad you are not my enemy, youngling. You are more dangerous by far than all your years times ten. Thus and so. We will need a bar of cold iron, forged in fire from old oak fresh fallen from a lightning bolt. And fennel stalks, the green still on them, many of them. The bar from thy hand alone, but the fennel I have in my stores. Get to it, youngling. Saint Lucia comes close, and it must be then! Get to it!"

* * *

FRIULI, ITALY – December 9th, 1854

"Thus and so. The iron is well forged youngling. Now, take the fennel, and plait three stalks together. Do not tear them!"

His hands moved, swift but sure.

"Good, good. Now, lay the plait along the iron, straight from tip towards the base. And then two more. Three..."

"Yes, old Mother. Yes." He smiled. "'For three is a magic number'. So you told me, and so I have read."

"Saccente." She grinned and smacked his head. "So much you know, you know it all, sì? Well, no, not now and not ever. But sì. Three is a number of power. Then plait three more, and wind them round and over the straight ones, each crossing the other, as the sun's path flies. Then three more, and wind those the same, but contrary to the sun. Thus, the straight path, the bright, and the dark."

* * *

The moon shone bright. "Three nights under the moon, youngling. Three nights, and you its guardian. Your eyes awake, all night and day, and your spirit steady. Do not sleep, or we must wait another year."

* * *

FRIULI, ITALY – Isola della Conna – December 13th, 1854

The night wind was cold. The green-swamp river was still, tempting any who dared to step on it, so it might feed on the ones who stepped. The old woman nodded. "Your hunt spoke true, youngling. Now, you remember the manner of the journey?"

He grimaced. "Blood. Blood and..." He flushed.

"Pfah. Yes. Blood and the fluid of your loins. Yes, yes, yes. Truly youngling, for all you have learned you still have much to learn. We go to Hell, and you blush at the going? I must as well. See? I have my own cold iron blade. Now. Blood first..."

* * *

"There. Wipe it over your eyes. Soon the night will change, and the Road will come."

He nodded, fingers busy. "And how must we travel? Do we fly? Do we walk? Are there dangers? What must I know?"

She shook her head. "Yes and yes? No and no? Absolutely, and none at all? I know not your path, your Truth. Each who travels finds their own. For some, a simple door. For another? Demons and dark, terror and blood. It is for your spirit to make the path. And yours will not be mine." The old woman shivered, and it was not the night wind's kiss that woke that shiver. "For me? I burn again, the witch fire and wood pile, the cold iron chain and the flames..."

He reached out, a hand to her shoulder. "Then stay here, old Mother. Tell me what I must do, and it will be done. You have done too much for me."

She sighed, her eyes sad. "No, youngling. The first time? The first can never be alone. If one who has not traveled is not with you, the door will not open—the Road will not come. So let us to it, for it must be done." The old woman smiled. "Now. Skin only this night, aye, and no blushing at my flesh's beauty!"

* * *

He bit down a scream. The bloody scars across his chest and back oozed, gaping. But his hand still wrapped tight round the iron bar. He looked around, but he was alone. Until the cold black air, soot-dust swirling in the wind, tore open. The old woman's hands batted the flames from her hair, her skin blistered and red. She spat. "Cazzo. I would not do this for many, youngling. Aye, and perhaps no more than one." She spat again. "Now. What do you think we do here this..." she looked up at a sky he knew was everblack, no moon or star hanging from it "... this night?"

"We hunt."

"Yes indeed. But what do we hunt?"

His lips opened. Then he bit them. He tilted his head, waiting.

She shook her head, grinning. "You make it worth doing, youngling. The Bruxa will find out, in time. No, our first prey we have. You know the path. Now you can travel it of your own doing or take another. The second? Well, we are here. Let us find us a witch, or mayhap more than one. Not yours, mind. She must not know what you can do. But others. The harvest was poor, and we must set it right. We find them, take what they bear, and return it to the World. You understand?"

"Aye. We hunt, we find—and kill!"

The old woman sighed. "Hunt? Yes. Find? So we hope, yes. Kill? Pfah. It is not so simple. Or the fire would have taken me and never let me go. But let us say yes. Kill. For this place and this moment, at least. For this hunt."

He nodded. He could feel it. No dagger was needed here. Muscles flexed, bones twisted—and no wolf, but a wolf that was a man, held tight a cold iron bar. "Yes old one." The words were growl, but the growl was words. "Let us hunt."

* * *

The woman screamed, her broom broken as the iron bar split it through. Split it—then landed hard on her head. The wolf that was not a wolf—the man who was not a man—took the sack she bore on her back,

80

opened it. Wolf teeth grinned. The harvest would be good the year to come.

* * *

One, two—six, seven, eight—and nine. Three times three the bar rose, the bar fell. Twelve, thirteen, fourteen, eighteen, nineteen, twenty. Twenty five and twenty six—and twenty seven. Three times three, and those threes times three. The sacks were heavy, but they were what they must be. He looked at the old woman. "And to return?"

She shrugged. "The same. Blood and..."

He sighed. "Of course. Blood 'and'." He shook his head. "Cannot you at least turn your back old Mother?"

She laughed. "Oh, youngling. You blush so sweetly."

* * *

FRIULI, ITALY – Isola della Conna – December 14th, 1854

"The packs? Where are they? Was our time wasted? What...?"

The old woman sniffed. "There were no packs, youngling. Or there were—one of those. They were, call them symbols. Call them magic. Call them anything you please. We gathered them, and they returned to the World. The harvest will wake, as the sun wakes, and the World will smile."

81

"I—I see." He half smiled, half shrugged. "Or I do not. One of those."

The old woman nodded. "Aye. One of those. Or both. It is ever thus, no?"

"By your words, old Mother and wise." He smiled—but did not try to dodge the slap across the ear.

She smiled too—then her eyes turned sad. "I have treasured my time with you youngling—more than many and many years I have lived. But now it is time."

"Time?"

"The Bruxa will find you here, aye, and with ease. And you are not ready—not yet. I can cloak your trail some, and I will. But you must do your part."

He raised an eyebrow, but waited, his own eyes sad.

She smiled, the ghost of a tear at one corner of an eye. "You learn well, young stregoni. You have heard, perhaps, how witches cannot cross running water? Well, it is of course sciocchezze, worse than the dribble on a babe's chin. If it were so, then I would not be here, or the many miles behind me anything but in front of me, and impossible to traverse. But, and you know it is the way, it is also true. For running water can smear the image of a spirit in a witch's view—aye, and a sorcerer's view–the same. And if a river may do this, then what of the ocean? Of the element of wild water itself? Well, it is so. So, to buy the time to become what you must, then you must put the wild ocean between the bitch and you. And there is a way. In Genova, there are boats–boats that sail to the New World, the far lands. A man with coin can find a berth, but a man with coin can be remembered. But there are always boats in need of crew.”

"Crew? But a sailor, I am none of. I…”

"You? You simply have more to learn.” The girl stood at the door. "And I can help. Pretty much whether you like it or not.” The girl whispered to the shadows behind her— shadows that spun, that twisted. Shadows that opened. Writhing tentacles pushed from the shadow-vortex and wrapped round not-Ellerimo’s head. His eyes shot wide—and closed.

* * *

GENOVA, ITALY – December 14th, 1854

"So. Mano del ponte you say? Well, certamente I could use one. Speak to my Bosun. If he thinks you’ll do, you’ll do. Your food, and half wages for the trip, sì? If you prove your worth, full wages for the return. Now, let us seal the matter with a drink. You, of course, pay. Oste! Another bottle! On my young crewman here! Yes, yes. I know. You have no coin. No matter. I will take it from your wages. Now drink with me! The New World waits, but the tide does not. Drink swift!”

* * *

The Captain watched his new crewman walk from the table. He waited, another candle-flickered, wine filled glass of passing time. Then he got up. He walked to the street, walked into a dark alley. "Was that as you wished?"

"No more, and no less." The girl who stepped from shadow handed him a small pouch. It clinked. "Of course, if you speak of this?" The girl raised one eyebrow.

The Captain nodded. There were tales told he had never believed—until the girl had shown him why he should. He shrugged. "Then I will be dead before a word leaves my lips signora. This I know."

"Then let it be so." The shadows twisted—and he knew he was alone.

* * *

Not-Ellerimo walked from the table, his steps weaving only slightly. The Bosun, he knew, would be no problem. The how of that 'no problem'? His head ached to even think of them, the tentacles. The thoughts. The knowledge. He shook his head, the ache real.

"It will pass." The alley was dark, the shadows thick in it. Which clearly suited the girl now standing in those same shadows. "Come here." And while there were few if any good reasons to walk into a dark alley in Genova, Not-Ellerimo knew this girl was one

84

he could not ignore. "Here." The girl held out her hand, two silver coins bright in her palm. "Not to spend."

Not-Ellerimo raised an eyebrow. "Then for?"

"You will know. When the time comes."

"I see."

"No. You do not. Not yet. But you will. And you will need this also." The girl held out a ring, one with a jewel that glowed no colour Not-Ellerimo had ever seen. "Put it on." Not-Ellerimo slid it on his finger. Muscles stretched, bones twisted—and more than bone, more than muscle. The girl waved her hand, and the air in front of Not-Ellerimo turned to mirror-glass. This time he—or rather she—raised both eyebrows. Half her height, he—or rather she—looked up at the girl. She grinned. "You see? Voice, body, nature? I wore it the night you were twice-born." The grin was gone. "You will need it."

Very-Not-Ellerimo sighed. "And if I ask you what that need might be?"

The girl grinned again. "Nope. Spoilers." She winked. "But if you want to... experiment? Then..." She winked again.

Very-Not-Ellerimo blushed. She pulled the ring from her finger. He blushed again. "I—think not."

The girl laughed. "Your loss. Now. Something you must know, if you are to use the ring. Once, long ago, it is said there was an ash tree. And some say Glooskap, and some say the hero Mikumwesu, his brother..."

* * *

"... and that is my tale, and that is what you should know."

Not-Ellerimo's brow furrowed. "So the ring is... I mean... Um, what do I mean?"

The girl shrugged. "Damned if I know. But that is the tale I was told. And now it is a tale you may tell if you find need or wish to tell it." Shadows twisted, and she was gone.

* * *

There should have been thunder. There should have been lightning tearing the skies and the very heavens weeping. There should have been portents and comets and demons of fire riding skeletal horses of ice-white bone—but there wasn't. What there was, was a ship, and an already distant harbour behind it growing smaller with every wind's breath. And ahead?

Ahead, more than the trees—waited.

Chapter 7

Strada dei gabbiani

THE SEA – March, 1855

Square rig, barque. Foremast, mizzen, main—yardarm, monkey's fist, parrel, pawl and baggywinkle. The words buzzed and bubbled, not one known to him ere-ever tentacles had sprung from shadows. But now? Now he knew each one, did Not-Ellerimo—each one and more. Aye, and new names also. 'Hey you', 'diego', 'swabby, 'gob' and 'tar', depending on who called him with more work to do, and whence they hailed. The name he'd given the Bosun? Gambani. Not that any ever used it. Fresh meat for the sea to suck on, like any new crew. None wished to know him, until ever he proved himself. And that was as he wished. 'Dimenticami' was the ship's name, a medium clipper made for cargo and passengers both, and Gambani? If none ever remembered him, Not-Ellerimo would think it well done. For he was followed still, that he knew, and wished to leave as few footsteps on the waves as he might for the Bruxa to chase. To hide among many might not fool those who followed, but it was at least a start.

And the sea itself might smear the traces of his passage.

* * *

THE SEA – April, 1855
Genova to Barcelona. Barcelona to Lisbon. Not-Ellerimo? He knew only water, until landfall. And then, each landing, more ropes, more cargo. Pull this out, put that in. Lumber and fine spices? Cloth and gold? He knew not, nor cared. He pulled ropes. In each harbour, he swabbed down decks licked by every wave when on the sea. Three decks the Dimentcami held, and a further deck, the forecastle, with houses for a galley and stores, and crew quarters with a small cabin abaft the main hatch. The first lower deck carried cargo also—two legged, with gold, in the two tiers of staterooms, each with eight berths. And two leg cargo with only coppers—the steerage, all crammed and mayhap two feet square to each of them. But steerage or stateroom, many days some cargo no longer walking, aye, or breathing either, was taken forth and fed to the waves around them. And every plank of every deck Not-Ellerimo knew, for who else to swab them down in the crew's twenty? Not the officers, and not the seasoned seamen. Who else but the new gob? Who else but 'diego'? And that also was exactly as he wished. For the lowest eyes, they saw the most if they were in heads that kept those eyes open. So

he swabbed each deck, and pulled each rope. And most of all—he waited.

And each day and day, day and day and day, above him the sky turned and gulls wheeled. Gulls—and more.

* * *

DERRY, IRELAND – May, 1855

"Amach as mo bhealach!" The man pushed past, his family behind, a wife and a daughter, their findings stacked and burdened. The man stopped, shook his head. "Boy! You! Where are the staterooms to be found?" Not-Ellerimo shrugged. "Non parlo inglese." He did—he had not wasted his time in ports. But none on the ship needed to know.

"Eeng-lazy? Pfah." the man spat. "Lazy English? Yes, they are. But it's no English, leathchcann. It's Gaeilge, for this is Derry, and this is Ireland." Not-Ellerimo made no move to avoid the slap that landed on his ear. He shrugged.

"I'm sorry sir. Have no mind to him. He's just deck-scum. It's the Bosun you need, sir. Allow me to take you?" Neither wise nor old, Aldo thought himself the first, and one who would never age. In every port he would only have to smile and the maids would come running. Aye, and oft times their Mothers the same. Aldo slapped Not-Ellerimo also. "This way sir. And you, bella signora." Aldo

89

motioned to the man's wife—but his smile was for the daughter. "This way."

Behind him, Not-Ellerimo swabbed deck, and nodded to himself. Sì. Sì, infatti. It was time. Or it would be... soon enough.

* * *

THE SEA – June, 1855
The sailor laughed. "Twenty Baiocchi you say? In silver? Hah! And where would you get such riches, gob?"

Not-Ellerimo shrugged. "Does it matter? I have it here." He opened his fist, the two silver coins bright. "One you bet him, the other you keep."

"And I must bet Aldo he cannot get the Irish girl on her back before we land? Idiota, you are. Aldo could get the Virgin Mary on her..." the sailor stopped, a look of fright on his face. He looked up. "Perdonami, Madonna!" The sailor spat. "You are a fool."

Not-Ellerimo shrugged again. "Then you know what they say. "Le persone stupide sprecano presto il loro denaro, sí?"

The sailor spat, but grinned. "Then yes, you are the fool—and your money is mine."

"But only when we near New Ireland, sí?"

"Si, sí. Qualunque cosa, gob. Now. Back to your mop, and quick about it!"

* * *

"E sarebbe un peccato, no?" Not-Ellerimo raised one eyebrow. The deck was empty, apart from the girl on the rail, her hand tight on a halyard. She turned her head, her eyes wild. While the night wind blew her long, unbound hair across her face, Not-Ellerimo knew those eyes were wet with many tears. He saw her fingers flex, begin to let go, the cold sea below waiting. "It was Aldo, yes?"

"An diabhal sin! No! Does the bastard parade me before the whole ship?" She spat. "No matter, then. If my Father hears or no, I will not be here to..." Her fingers flexed again, the rope loosening.

Not-Ellerimo sighed. He shook his head. "As I said. It would be a shame, no? To let him win? And the water..." he nodded towards the sea below "... it is dark, yes? At least let me show you what waits, yes?"

"Pfah. You think to stop me? Show me your water, amadán, and I will welcome my grave."

Not-Ellerimo shrugged, and turned his body from the wind. He reached into the pouch at his waist, then held what he took from it cupped in his hands. He whispered, and a flame flickered to its tip. Then he held the Hand of Glory high, no wind disturbing it in the frozen scrap of time it called. He sighed. Then, the corpse-candle tight in hand, he threw a rope round the girl's waist, so that he would not touch her, and used it to pull her to the deck. As she slumped down, her hand slid down the halyard, fingers still wrapped around it. Not-Ellerimo tied the rope short against the rail, then wrapped a cloth round his hand, reached and un-clenched her fingers. He took another rope, and tied it round her other hand, then removed the cloth from his hand and wrapped it with the rope. He pulled the rope tight so his hand touched hers. As he touched her, she started to life.

"Let go of me! What, you seek Aldo's leavings? Fuck tú, a mhuc! You..."

Not-Ellerimo took a coin from his pocket, showed it to her. Then he flipped it, took his hand away—the coin hanging mid-spin in the air. He raised an eyebrow.

"What..." The girl fell silent. She looked around, at a rope on the rail curled in a wind that did not blow, that she could not hear, still and solid in air from which it should be falling. "Draoidheachta!"

Not-Ellerimo shrugged. "Witchcraft? No." His eyes grew distant, remembering. He smiled. "Whatever you wish to believe. But no matter. I think we may be able to help each other."

"I may be ruine... I may be Aldo's leavings, but no! I will not take the devil's aid for..."

"Devil? If I was il diavolo, would I be on this wretched vessel, swabbing decks and everyone's servant?"

"But..." the girl pointed at the Hand of Glory.

"Yes, yes, yes. It is a tool, only that. Was its making gruesome? Perhaps. Did it require deeds some would not count honourable? Even so. But still. A tool. While we touch, none may see us, or know of us." He remembered old Mother's words. "Well, mostly none. But still. I think we may be of use to each other, you and I. May we discuss the matter?"

"Use?" The girl's eyes were less scared—more calculating. She looked at the Hand—looked at him. "Perhaps you are not a witch. Perhaps I do not care. Say on, sir?"

Not-Ellerimo looked up. No gulls circled, as they would not if they were gulls. But not all gulls were truly gulls. "Not here. Will you come with me, and not let go of my hand?"

The girl smiled, her first, though the smile shivered. "Well sir. You ask near as sweet as Aldo. Though..." she spat "... I hope not with his intent. You may remove the rope. I'll not let go."

* * *

The Captain's cabin door had, of course, been locked. But the corpse-candle in hand, it mattered not. The fire within glowed red, but sat frozen, not dancing. Still, the room was warm. Not-Ellerimo poured a cup of the open wine bottle on the table next to where the Captain lay frozen in his bed. He passed it to the girl. "So. If I may, there are matters to discuss. Matters that are, some would say, delicate?"

The girl raised both eyebrows. She lifted the hand still clasped in Not-Ellerimo's, waved it at the Hand in his other. "Delicate? I think we are past delicate sir. Pfah. Sir. What is your name?"

Not-Ellerimo shrugged, his eyes distant. "Name? I have had many. For now? For here? Call me Gambani. But no matter."

"Caitlin." the girl spat, her spittle hanging in the air as it left her mouth. "Euggh. Though I should change it. For pure I am not, and maybe never was, or I'd never have given way to..."

"Pfah. Sciocchezze, damigella. For nonsense is what it is. For humans, are not such things natural?"

"Er—humans?"

"No matter. We will get to that. But still, yes. Aldo. He is no honour to his Father's name, but then, he never knew his Father. So there is that. But let me save you your blushes. There was Aldo. And he is charming, or so I am told. And he..."

"He charmed me? Yes, if you put it that way. And I have no blushes for it. He charmed me, and I went with him, and we lay together, and my skirts came up for him and..."

"Quite. And. But..."

"Let me fucking finish! I swear, men! You have no idea! He did what he did, and he finished in me! And I am broken, and my

Mother, she inspects me once each week! Not because not being broken means I have never been—well, *been*. But because stupid *men* think so, and my Father seeks to marry me to money! And my Mother, she will see me broken, and if she waits long enough see more than that! I'm sure Aldo has left more behind him than tears in every port he lands in. I..."

"Hush, girl. Hush. I..."

"Hush? *Hush*?" The girl stopped. She looked at the Hand. "That means none may hear us, yes?"

"Si."

"THEN DON'T YOU FUCKING HUSH ME, YOU STUPID FUCKING MAN! You cannot know what it means to a gir..."

"Ah. Man. Yes. About that." Under the table, agile fingers slipped the ring he had been given onto a finger. Muscles twisted, bones creaked. But Very-Not-Ellerimo made sure she never let go of the girl's hand.

"Wha... WHAT?"

"If I may?"

"D... Diabhal." The girl's whisper was ragged.

Very-Not-Ellerimo sighed. "Have we not been there already?" She peered up over the table. "Can we perhaps...?" she nodded to the Captain's day couch. The two got up, each not letting go of the other's hand. They sat. "That, I confess, is better. No. I am not a devil. Not—well. There are many things I am

95

not. But if I may, let me ask you a question. If you were my friend…"

"Me?"

"Well, you and all your people."

"*My* people?"

Very-Not-Ellerimo sighed. "No matter. If you were my friend, would it not be good for that friendship for me to know, to learn, as much as I may about you?"

"Well, I suppose yes."

"And if you were my enemy?"

"Then absolutely yes."

"And if I did not know if you were to be friend or enemy, but knew we must live close?"

"Well then, I suppose twice yes. But what… how…?"

"There is a land to which this vessel travels. And those it brings think them new owners of that land, where none were before. But there were people there long before you new folk arrived. And there were others there long before those L'nu'k who your people found there, L'nu'k your kind too often set aside. And one of those? Long, long ago as your folk count long, the Mikumwessuk were created from the bark of an ash tree. It is a long tale, but then…" Very-Not-Ellerimo glanced at the Hand "… we have time to tell it. So. Once it was, and this is what was once…."

* * *

"So you are—what did you say? 'Mikumwessuk'?"

Very-Not-Ellerimo shrugged. "I did not say that. I simply told you a tale, no?"

"But…"

"But? But no matter. Pfah. Are there not many tales? Is Truth in one of them, or many? All of them or none? This I will say, not one of them will set you unbroken when next your Mother examines you. And not one of them will make undone what was or was not done when Aldo finished his play inside your eager body."

Caitlin flushed. "Yes. Eager, that I cannot deny. But then, there is nothing that may be done. I am…"

"You are? This I will say. You are whatever you choose to make you, whoever you choose to be." Very-Not-Ellerimo took the pouch from her belt. "Three things I have here. This…" she showed Caitlin the fire glass blade, "… and this" she lifted a small glass bottle "… and this." Another bottle. "Let me show you the blade." And Very-Not-Ellerimo set the blade to the skin of her arm. She drew it gently forward—and a layer of skin, as thin almost as the very glitter of sun on a spider web, lifted clean from her flesh. She held it up. "The second bottle? It is a glue. A glue not made to set paper or leather, but one that will set skin and flesh as though they were ever one. A skin and flesh your Mother will seek and see and see not one thing to set her thoughts awry."

Caitlin stared close. "And the third?"

"The third? That will set any matter of Aldo aside, and your moon-time not one moment before or after it must come."

Caitlin looked at Very-Not-Ellerimo. She shrugged. "I was set to kill myself. If your deeds kill me, then I am hardly the loser. But why?"

"Why?"

"Why would you do this for me?"

"Well, it is said, yes? Tutto ha un prezzo? That all things, they have a price? And yes. I have mine. It is thus. Your Father, he is a man of short temper, si?"

"Short? No shorter than the gap between two sheets of paper. Why?"

"Well, thus and so. It would be better for what I must do if I had never been on this vessel. So, perhaps, what if some lowly crew-gob took a thing of value from your family's cabin? And you saw them, and told your Father, and told him he could catch them?"

"Why, then he would do so! And most likely strangle you with his bare hands!"

"Well then. Or perhaps, in the struggle... well. Then who knows, yes?"

"Yes. But..."

"But me no buts Signora. Might we have an agreement?"

"Then—then yes."

"Well then. Let the matter be done. And done as it must. Lie down. And lift me your skirts."

* * *

THE SEA – July, 1855

"Athair, I saw him! The one they call Gambani! He went in our cabin, and he took it! Your picture—Seanmháthair!"

"Wha.... Where is he? The bastard! Call me the Captain!"

"Daidí, no! It was but moments gone! You can catch him! He went to the deck!"

Caitlin ran after her Father as he headed for the upper deck. And as he—she?—had said it would be, it was so. Gambani was towards the side rail, the picture clutched in one hand. She watched as her Father ran to him, his fists raised. "Give that to me, bastard! Give it..." Her Father grabbed him, struggled. Somehow the two slipped. Her Father fell to the deck, the picture in his hand. Of Gambani? One last splash—and he was gone.

* * *

"I see sir. Or perhaps..." the Captain's eyes narrowed, glinted "... perhaps there is in fact nothing *to* see." The Captain looked at the Bosun. "Your thoughts?"

The Bosun shrugged. "As you wish. There will be some numbers to correct in the ship's accounts."

The Captain tilted his head. "How much?"

99

"Perhaps I tallied some columns wrong. Say—five lira?"

The Captain looked at Caitlin's Father. "My Bosun's English is not always perfect. As with his columns and adding. I believe he meant, shall we say, one sovereign?" Caitlin's Father blanched but nodded. "I see. As, I am sure, will my crew once the Bosun has spoken with them. Now. What was it you wished to talk of sir?"

Caitlin's Father nodded once. "Oh, simply to thank you for an excellent voyage. And to ask if that is indeed St John we see come close?"

"It is indeed sir. And it has been a pleasure to have you with us."

* * *

The sea swelled, the land close. The wolf, a dagger plunged deep in his chest, paddled hard. And behind him, three gulls tilted wings and slid down onto the wind.

Chapter 8

Strangers on a shore

SIKNIKT, NEW IRELAND – July, 1855

The wolf paddled hard. Had some seen it, that would have been no strangeness. The rope around its middle? The leather pack strung to the rope? And the dagger deep in its chest? That, yes. Strange and stranger.

The wolf paddled—swift and hard. The land reached out into the ocean, but the lighthouse at its tip, lights beginning bright as the dusk fell, was no place the wolf sought. He paddled, seeking the trees. As the land curved North, the trees crept closer to the sea. And the lighthouse well behind him, the wolf set to shore. From the waves it walked, seawater fleeing fast from his thick outer coat, the soft undercoat warm and dry beneath. It fell to its side, not from exhaustion, but from need. A paw rose, a claw—and the dagger pulled from its chest, the wound closing tight as each fraction of the blade slid clear. Not-Ellerimo darted eyes left and right, to the sea, to the sky—and to the woods. He set the blade back to his thigh, and it was gone. Clothes only ever came after the dagger. He had gathered new ones from the ship before his 'off-boarding'—the old had been left in the water when he fell from the ship. He dressed, swiftly.

"Pfah. You should not have wasted your time." A rabbit coming out of a forest was no strange thing. But one that talked? Not-Ellerimo's hand slipped to the dagger hilt. "No. You need no clothing, meat. You are mine this night." The rabbit warped, shifted—and the Bruxa laughed. "Yes, I see your dagger, meat. Use it as you will. That is why I brought my sisters with me." Two more rabbits hopped from the wood. They warped—shifted. "One wolf, sisters. Surely we shall not bear defeat!" The three Bruxa laughed—and three bears roared. Not-Ellerimo reached to his thigh, pulled the dagger. He aimed for his chest–perhaps, he knew, for the last time.

The howl that split the night was like none he had ever heard. And the huge grey wolf that ran from the forest was like none he had ever seen. The wolf hammered into the three bears, bowling one clear, setting jaws to a second. In a moment, the third roared, swelled, and one massive, clawed paw batted the grey wolf from its prey. The wolf yowled once, loud. Twice, and louder. A third call the wolf sent and was answered. Because the very sky, the very air, burned redder than any hell.

* * *

Not-Ellerimo coughed. He ran a hand over hair frizzled from flame. He looked down at clothes more black burned char than cloth, to the front of him, where three crisped, charred lumps sat at the forest's edge. He looked up. Wolves do not grin—but the huge grey one in front of him grinned wide. It warped, shifted. And no wolf, but a naked girl, stood in its place. He coughed again. "Lu… lupo mannaro. My thank…"

The naked girl shook her head, ran her hands over parts of her Not-Ellerimo tried not to look at. "First, in case you didn't notice, there isn't one inch of man about me. And second, I…" The girl spits. "Pfah. Humans! Your words are so *empty*! But I'm not a werewolf anyway. Can we change the subject? It's embarrassing."

Not-Ellcrimo raised an eyebrow. "Empty? What do you mean? I saw a wolf. I see a girl. And my thanks for your aid. But..?"

The naked girl spat again. "I mean *empty*. What you said. Werewolves. Yuck." The girl grimaced. "Look, werewolves are humans who sometimes get lucky enough to be wolves. I'm a wolf. It's just that sometimes I have to suffer being human. I am not a bloody werewolf! Tell him, Darek!"

"As Katya speaks, so verily it is." The deep voice rumbled both soft and loud, like mountains speaking to a stormy sky. Not-Ellerimo looked round for the source, saw nothing. The naked girl laughed and pointed. Up. And as Not-Ellerimo's eyes followed her finger, the dragon closed wings and dropped to the shore. It warped, flexed—and a man was there. Not tall, not short. Black hair blowing in the wind, but nothing much to look at. Until Not-Ellerimo looked in his eyes. Grey, like the clouds that scudded across the sky, but with flecks one moment blue, and another red. Eyes that knew how to smile, like they were doing, but even when they did, held pain. "Play nice, Katya." The man looked at Not-Ellerimo. "A... let us say, a friend, told us you might need some help. We were here looking for..."

"I'm <u>sure</u> I smelled her Darek! Father *told* me, and..."

The man grinned. "And told you there would be rabbits, perhaps? Hmmm?"

Katya blushed. "Weeeell—*may*beeee."

The man laughed. "Well, as it may be, so let it be." He looked at Not-Ellerimo. "But no. She is not as Thiess was. She is..."

Not-Ellerimo started. "Thiess? You knew him?"

The man called Darek shrugged. "No. But May... I mean, the Shadow Child, she told us of him. She said you would face more than one blade could handle. And when the Shadows ask, one does not say no. So here we are."

Not-Ellerimo let no sign come to his face. But he heard. Shadows. So...

Darek laughed. "Yes. There are two. The Child and—well. 'And'. But Katya is a wolf and I am…"

"You? You are strange. If you were atookwokun of my people, chepĕchealm you would be, and I would seek the booöin who called you, served you, and…" The old woman who stepped from the forest was small, the height of a man's waist.

Darek raised an eyebrow. "And? And slay me, as Noojekĕsĭgŭnodăsĭt did?"

The old woman raised both eyebrows. "So. You know our tales, it seems."

Darek bowed his head. "Some, perhaps. I may be older than I look. But…"

Katya laughed. "Older? Mother…" she looked at the old woman "You say tepknuset, I think? Well, Mother woke me maybe—a million years ago? I don't know. I lose count. But I'm just a girl. Darek? He's really old. He was here beforc 'here' was! When the Wheel turned for the old here and made it new! Anyway. I'm a wolf. Well, most of the time. Wolves are simple. Darek—Darek's complicated."

Darek raised a hand. "Enough, Katya. If the wise one is to be nitap, then we should show respect." He nodded to the old woman, who was most clearly not any woman. "Your stories are yours. They are not mine to tell, or mine to set aside. But may I tell you mine?"

The old woman nodded.

Darek nodded again. "My thanks. We come from where we were, and though we stand here together, that does not mean the paths we took here must be the same. Nor must what was, for each of us, be what was for each other. Though tepknuset, peskewiku's, apuknajit—aye, each and more—are not Arianrhod? Well, then they are not. And still—they are. For all tales are true, to those who know them true. And they do not make others false. So this? This is mine. Old it is, and older still, and older than those olds, each one. But thus it was, and thus it is. Around fires on cold nights, it is called 'Dragon's Tear Wine'. For me? Well...

Chapter 9
Dragon's Tear Wine

A LAND THAT WAS – Before the Wheel turned

*He wasn't a thief. Thieves were two-a-pick-the-negotiable-currency of-your-choice. What he was, was a **successful** thief. And there were a lot less of those than people knew about. As in, none at all. After all, if people knew you were a thief, it mostly meant you'd been caught. Which, to him, meant by definition you weren't very good at it. Of course, there was Sartil ShadowCast. They said he'd stolen the Great Crown of Atuth-Khan right off the Khan's head while he was holding court. People said Sartil had the power to wrap himself in shadows, so nobody could see him. And everyone knew stories about Greta Greymist. A thief who could turn herself into—well, into grey mist, and pour through the smallest hole. That, they'd say, was how she'd got into the Tomb of the Lost Prince, and got out with the Eye of the Wind. And the tales of Ulfir Unseen, who had the power of invisibility. Like the time he'd stolen every stitch of the Queen of Sarakir's* *robes while she bathed. Aye, and some said her virtue too. He'd heard every story. Hells, he'd written most of them. Because the thing about Sartil, and about Greta, even Ulfir? The thing was, even though everyone knew about them, and what they'd done, they didn't exist.*

*The thief smiled. He'd got a good price for the Great Crown, and for the Eye. And the Queen of Sarakir had paid a small fortune for someone—**anyone**—to take her virtue. When your family's the result of centuries of inbreeding you have to take the rough with the smooth. Even if you **are** a Queen.*

But that was it. Because the most important thing about being a successful thief wasn't being able to wrap yourself in shadows, or turn into mist, or invisible. It was something harder than that. It was being places where there were things worth stealing. Being there—but not existing at all. Or not being remembered, because the only thing people saw was something else. Like now. Right now the thief wasn't existing, because a rock was. Or the shadow of a rock. Because he wasn't just a thief. He wasn't even just a successful thief. He was, he thought modestly, the most successful thief ever.

And he didn't exist.

"People tell me you can see the future." The merchant the thief hadn't been following, though an old priest, a passing

deer and, right now, the shadow of a rock might have had different opinions on the matter if asked, was rich. Which was why the thief 'hadn't' been following him. "They say they give you gold, and you drink potions, and you tell what will come. And that afterwards you can't remember what you spoke." *The merchant looked down his nose at the ragged beggar.* "I've heard of people like you. They're called drunks."

"And do they say, these people, they ever regretted giving me gold? Did they say the poison I told them they would put in their brother's wine would work, and it did not? Or that the will their brother had written was not where I told them it would be? Or that the will I told them they would leave in its place, that left all their brother owned to them alone, was not believed? Did they tell you that, Keldir, son of Marduk, brother of Torfan, blessed be his memory?"

"You're nothing but a fool, Blood. My brother isn't dead."

"Indeed not." *The beggar smiled.* "Not yet."

"Pfah. I..."

"Yes?"

The shadow of a rock saw the merchant spit, and throw a heavy pouch in front of the beggar. A pouch that clinked. The shadow had heard a lot of clinks in its time, and this clink, he thought, sounded yellow. Profitably yellow.

The beggar picked up the pouch. He picked it up, and took glass vials from his rags and mixed them, and he drank what he mixed. He drank it, and his eyes glazed, and he spoke of a particular poison, and a glass of wine. And he spoke of a loose brick in a house, and a day the house would be empty. And he spoke of a merchant whose business had been failing, who inherited new businesses and whose pockets got heavy with gold. And then the beggar turned his head, and he looked at the shadow of a rock that stood near, and he said something new. He said "You will find what you seek and lose what you have. And in that losing you will be made greater, and in that greatness you will have what you seek."

Now another thing about a successful thief is, they should know what's worth stealing and what isn't. And while the prattle of a beggar telling a rich merchant what he wants to hear isn't worth a bent copper coin, the magic a beggar uses to tell a true future would be worth more gold than even the shadow of a rock had ever stolen. But the thief didn't know which kind of words the beggar had spoken. So instead of following the beggar, and taking the beggar's gold as he'd planned, he followed the merchant instead. Or at least a stray dog, an old woman, and a flash of sunlight seen out of the corner of a merchant's eye did. And soon the stray dog and the old woman and the flash of sunlight, they didn't follow a rich merchant. They followed an even richer merchant, who wept over his brother's recent death by day, and counted his brother's gold by night—when he wasn't 'comforting' his brother's rather attractive widow. And the thief decided maybe the beggar's tongue didn't just prattle after all.

So the thief took some of his stolen gold, and bought rich clothing and put it on, because not existing had its price, and rocks and stray dogs don't wear clothes. Then he took more of his gold, and filled a pouch. And he went looking for the beggar. Or rather, the thief didn't—but a very rich merchant did. And the beggar didn't seem too unhappy to be found.

"So. You've come."

The thief didn't know who the beggar thought he was, but he didn't care. He threw a heavy bag that clinked its own sweet clinkiny down on the ground. "Cease your prattle, rags. Tell me..."

"Tell you what? And who should I tell? The rich merchant you pretend to be, who has no future because he has no past? Or the thief you are, who has a past, but no future?"

The thief knew the beggar was on to him. But the thing with not existing at all is to exist as something else, and never to stop. Right now, he was a rich merchant, and rich merchants do not like being taken for fools. "I see. Those who told me of you must have thought me witless. I'll..."

"You'll what? Walk away, and take off your robes? Become a passing soldier, or a vagrant breeze, and follow me? Sneak silent into my home to steal my secrets? Come. We are not fools, you and I. There is nothing you ever decided to steal you have not taken. So why should either of us waste time, or foolish effort? I know when I'm beaten. I'll give you freely what you seek to take! Walk with me, thief."

"You'll give it to me?"

"Why not? What I have, I'll not lose. And what I have has told me I won't die of giving it to you. So why should I care if you have it too?"

"And if you're wrong? If I kill you anyway, once I have what I seek?"

The beggar smiled. "Then you won't have it at all—because if it lied to me, my secret, to my death—how could you ever trust it for yourself? Come."

So the thief followed the beggar, and he followed him a ways out of town to a cave. Inside the cave the beggar showed the thief how he lived there, and any nook or cranny the thief asked about, the beggar showed him what was in it.

"So, thief. You've asked me every question you could ask, but not the one you looked for me to steal an answer for. So ask!"

The thief shrugged. "So, old man. Is it true? Can you see the future?"

The beggar smiled. "No. Not at all. But I can drink it!" And he touched a rock near him, and the rock faded and turned into a table. A table with an empty jug on it. He picked up the jug, and he filled it with water from a bucket. Then he took from inside his rags a stone. And the stone, its colour swirled stormy grey, and strange lights danced in it, sometimes blue and sometimes red. "You see this stone, thief? I can promise you've never seen one like it." And the thief shook his head. There was little he didn't know of gems and precious metal, for the only thing he loved more than stealing such things was to craft them into new shapes and forms. And this stone was like none he'd ever seen. Then the beggar dropped the stone into the water. For a while it fizzed, red drops spilling from it until the water was as red as any wine. The beggar reached into the pitcher and took out the stone. "And if I drank that wine, then a thousand tomorrows I'd see. Not the future, but the many futures, because there are no promises, thief. Only what may be, and the path to follow to reach each one. But many will give gold to know those paths, won't they?"

"I suppose they would."

"Oh, they do. But—well. To all things there's a price. A thief must know that, yes?"

The thief, he said nothing. But his eyes never left the stone in the beggar's hands.

"Aye. I see where you look. But look close, light fingers. Do you see, the stone is smaller? And smaller it gets, each time it's used. And smaller, and smaller—and what then? For when it is gone, it is gone. And this I'll tell you. There's no other gem like this in all the world. Not now."

The thief smiled. "The world's a big place, old man. Perhaps more of your stone can be found."

"Well, if it was a stone, perhaps you'd be right. But of course, it isn't."

"So what is it?"

"You see the red that comes from it when it sits in the water? What do you think that red is?"

"Magic?"

"Heh. If magic were a colour, then every child would paint their Mother rich. No indeed. It is tears."

"Tears?"

"Aye. You see, once there were things in this world that are no more. Things from the birthing of the world, with the world's power in them. And as their eyes had opened with the world's first breath, they saw every breath to come, and every moment. And they wept. Because few of those moments brought smiles, and most were filled with blood, and men killing other men. And every land has memories of these creatures, in every tongue ever spoken. Eskilya duskalen they called themselves— people of the scale. But men—they called *them dragons. And those tears wept into the water? Those are the Dragon's Tears. And the stone that weeps them, that is the Dragon's Eye."*

"An amusing tale, old man. But let me pretend to believe it. Surely to replace what you have, all you need is a dragon!"

"Indeed. But there lies my problem. Because this eye? This eye is the second eye of the last dragon. One I slew a thousand, thousand years gone."

*"A problem indeed. Though even you do not look **that** old."*

The beggar laughed. "Oh, I've more secrets than one, light hands. Many more. The blood in a man can serve another well if that other has the right blade knowledge. But you've marked the problem well. For I need a dragon, and a dragon can't be had. Unless..."

"Unless?"

"Well, unless one has a greedy thief!" The beggar waved his hands, and the thief found he couldn't move a single muscle even a single finger's width. The beggar's magic had him bound. The beggar went to the back of the cave and dragged forward a small, scared boy. He grinned. "Your new home, thief. But don't worry—it won't be yours for long. I just need your body to be a little more—cooperative." The beggar reached out his hand to the young boy, and his hand sank into the boy's body. As he pulled it back, the boy screamed—and went limp.

"You see, a body cannot hold two souls. And yours...?" the beggar reached his hand again, and it sank into the thief. He pulled. "Well, yours must take a new home for a while." This time it was the thief who screamed, and his sight went black. When it returned, the first thing he saw—was his own limp body. The beggar smiled down at him. "You see, a careful man may sip the Dragon's Tears. And sip indeed, for the spirit of the dragon enters him, and the dragon's Sight, and the many futures he'll see. But to see that seeing? Well. For a time, he must forget himself, and remember only the dragon." The beggar poured from the pitcher into a wine pouch. "But if the man is not a careful man, but a greedy one, then he won't just sip, will he? He'll gulp. And then the spirit of the dragon will fill the man whole, and he'll forget all he ever was." And the beggar filled the thief's body's mouth, and touched the thief's body's throat, and the throat swallowed. And the beggar poured and touched, touched and poured. Then he looked down at the not-young not-a-boy. "But a man who has forgotten he is a man? Whatever he may be, he is not a dragon. He is but a man. He has a man's heart, a man's life—and a man's spirit. Unless—well, unless there is some seed, some part of a dragon in him. A seed which might grow, if enough years pass. To eat that man's heart and make it a true dragon's." The beggar went and touched a

third rock, and it faded. He opened a box carved with strange runes, and took out a bloody mass. "I took this from the last dragon. For a day like this. My magic has kept it like the moment I took it, and you see, still it beats! I regret, you probably like your meat cooked, but that would spoil the casting." The beggar took hold of the heart, and picked up a rune carved knife. He took the knife, and plunged it into the thief's body, cutting deep and cutting it open. Then the beggar forced the bloody mass in his hand into the thief, into his rib cage. The beggar reached into the young boy's body, and took hold. The body screamed, and the thief's eyes went blind. But when his sight returned, it was in more familiar eyes.

And the thief—who was no thief anymore—screamed also.

Then the beggar laughed, and the laugh was cold. "You should be grateful, thief! The heart still holds blood, and if blood has great power, a dragon's is greater! It will heal you, give you years longer than men know. And then many more! Because blood may be years, but the heart is life, and this heart is a dragon's heart, and your days will be a dragon's count of days as you change. And change you will! From man to dragon? Aye. And from dragon to man also. And I want you to live those many years, thief. Because you are not yet what I need. But each time you change to scale, it will be some small harder to change from scale to man. Until? Well. Truly, until. For there will come—a time when you are, that I seek, and never will you shed scale again. And if that time has no swift coming? Well then. I have a knife, and I know its use. I can find other blood, other hearts. Wait for me, duskalen-to-be. And when I come, your eyes will be mine, and your blood mine—and your heart!

Chapter 10

Into the woods

SIKNIKT, NEW IRELAND – July, 1855

"... and that is the tale of the wine of the Dragon's tear." The one called Darek bowed to the old woman. "And if you wish, if ever the time should come, let it be yours to tell, as the tale of Noojekĕsĭgŭnodăsĭt is yours. So that we know, each of us, our truths do not set the truths of others aside, as theirs do not cast our own into the void either. Yes?"

The old woman smiled. She tilted her head, one eyebrow raised. "E'e. Or moque—who knows how the sun may rise, or how it sets." She smiled again and nodded. "Etugjel, chepĕchealm-to-be. Etugjel."

Not-Ellerimo coughed. "I... well, here I was, and here I stand. And my thanks for that standing, wise ones. And—well." He blushed, trying not to look at—well, at places. "And wolf-one..."

Katya raised an eyebrow. "I see. So I am not a wise one then? Only a wolf-one?"

Not-Ellerimo blushed even more red. "No! No, I meant... I mean..."

"Do not tease, Katya. He is..."

"Yes Darek. I know. He is. But he's cute! Like a rabbit!"

Not-Ellerimo flinched. "Rabbit? Are you going to...?" His hand dropped to his thigh, the dagger within his flesh.

"Eat you, little rabbit?" Katya shook her head. But she grinned. "No. You aren't my..." She grinned wider "... my type of meat."

Not-Ellerimo let go of the dagger. "Then my thanks wolf... er..."

Katya smiled. "Katya. Try it. It's easy."

Not-Ellerimo blushed. "My thanks indeed, Katya. And..." Not Ellerimo bowed to the naked man. "... and to you also, Darek. The Bruxa has been seeking my life as long as I have lived. It is good that she is..."

"Dead, young booöin? Were it only so simple. The puowin—what is it you say? The Bruxa? The witch? No. She is not dead."

Not-Ellerimo's eyes darted in every direction they could find, and perhaps ten more. He turned to the old woman. "But... how...?" He pointed to the charred remains. "Old... I mean, um, wise... I mean..." He pointed at the remains again.

The small old woman, a shape Not-Ellerimo knew from a ring still in his pouch, laughed. "Gewaqsing"

"Ge-wa... I am sorry, old..."

The old woman laughed again. "You are close. Gewaqsing. Try it..." the old woman smiled and nodded to Katya. "As the wolf said, it is not so hard. It is not my name, but it will fare as one for your mouth."

"Ge-Gewaqsing. My thanks, wise one. But..." Not-Ellerimo nodded to the charred remains.

The Mikumwessuk woman nodded. "E'e. The chepĕchealm burned them with his fire, indeed. But the puowin? They do not die so easily. They... it is, metue'g? It is hard to say, because as he says..." Gewaqsing nodded to Darek "... your truths are not the truths of my people. Not that yours are false, or mine either. But your path must follow your truth, until you become part of ours." Gewaqsing shrugged, and looked at Darek.

"It is as the wise one..." at Darek's words, the old woman chuckled. Darek smiled, but bowed his head. "As the *wise one* says. Behind each truth that walks the land is another, and behind that, perhaps another and another. Until there is a Truth, maybe, we never find—or maybe not even that. But we must each walk the path of our own truth, until we reach where that path takes us. So no. I regret, the witches? The Bruxas, as you say? They are not dead."

Not-Ellerimo sighed. "E così va." He turned, looked out over the sea. "So many waves. And still I must run? Is this my life?"

Darek nodded. "Of course. We never stop running, not one of us. Whether our feet move fast or slow. But whether we run is not the choice. The choice is which direction we take."

Not-Ellerimo sighed again. "Thus and so. The witches. You say they are not dead.

But how... how do they still live? After you set them with your fire, lucertola grande...?" he nodded to Darek "By your claws and...?"

Katya laughed. "Lizard? He called you a lizard, Darek! Should I claw him?"

Darek smiled. "Be still, Katya. But, um..." he looked at Not-Ellerimo, and raised an eyebrow. "Lizard?"

Not-Ellerimo blushed. "My apologies. It is hard, when one knows there are no such things as dragons."

Katya smiled. But the smile was ice. "I see. Nor are there wolves who must suffer being two legs, or Bruxas who may change shape, or..." she nodded to Gewaqsing "... or wise children of Mikumwessu. It is true, is it not? Ask any stupid human who walks these lands and they will tell you. I..."

"Katya. No matter." Darek sounded tired. "It is..."

"No Darek. Not this time." Katya spat. "*You* know, even if this not-wolf does not. You know there is a world that was, that you knew, before the world was what it is now. Just as there is a world I knew when Mother made me. Just as there is a world those here knew, and know still, where Glooskap walked! To deny these things is to walk in darkness. This one? He must see." She glared at Not-Ellerimo. "A blind wolf, or even one not-wolf? That one does not run far or run for long, youngling."

Not-Ellerimo settled his hand on his thigh. "I will run as far as I must. Si, and as long, to cast the Bruxa down. What is it, this thing I must see?"

Gewaqsing shook her head at Not-Ellerimo. "Did you not ask?"

"Ask?"

"She told me, the Shadow Girl. Of the one named Caterina? Three hundred years she told you she had walked. And you did not ask her how?"

"I..." not-Ellerimo's eyes filled with tears. "I... she was... But she left me! She..."

Gewaqsing shrugged. "Left you? If that is your truth, then I suppose it must be so. But it is not the truth I was told. That she walked a path of night black and red blood? E'e. That she sowed seeds of chaos all about her, so you might have this chance to be... whatever it is you will be? E'e. That she lived years, and more years, and years much more than that? E'e, for that can be the way of Puowi-ni\'skw. But, as it was, so must it be. Yet, you did not ask her, of those long years and their making. And if you do not know how such a one may live those years? Well then. How can you know how to end them?"

"You are wise, donna saggia. Do you know this thing?"

"I? I cannot. It is not my story, do you see? On the path I walk, in my Truth, there is an answer. But my path is not yours, and my Truth is not yours either. So the answers I know are not the answers you must seek. But tell me. Do you know nothing? Did those who taught you show you no path?"

"I... Thiess, he spoke of the hunting. The Benandanti, they would take their spirits to Hell, that they might seek out witches and return the year's harvest. My heart-Mother, she showed me the manner of it."

"And did you kill them, your prey, in this Hell you speak of?"

"Why, yes. Or rather, no. Or..." Not-Ellerimo's eyes glazed as he sought memory. "... or, perhaps, both. They died in Hell, but not forever. As my heart-Mother burned in the witch fire but was with me so many years later."

Gewaqsing nodded. "And? Hunt, young wolf. Hunt your Truth!"

"And so it is, that Bruxas, the dark witches, they may die, but not die. But still, they flee from peril." Not-Ellerimo's left eye narrowed, a hunter on the path. "So it is not so simple."

Gewaqsing smiled. "Is it ever?"

"No indeed. But yes, and yes twice! For they fear peril, even though it seems they may not die, even if they live when they are rended. So.... Soooooo..."

"So?"

"So there is more Truth to be found!" Not-Ellerimo nodded. "I must hunt me a witch!"

"To do what?"

"To rend the secret from them!"

"How? Will you set your claws to them and threaten them with their ending?"

"Yes!" Not-Ellerimo's face fell. "But, well, no. They will live. None will tell me how to end them, because if I do not know, I cannot truly hurt them."

The Mikumwessuk nodded, slowly. "So. You must hunt one who has Truth, but is not threatened by giving you that Truth, but one you may give reason to offer it."

Not-Ellerimo's eyes lit up. "Stregoni! Heart-Mother, she told me! That if I was not a witch, I must be a sorcerer, one who learned secrets to set power to my hand, if that power was not mine by nature. Like, what was it she said? Like a man who may not run, but knows how to sit a horse and set it swift to carry him! And she said... she said... she said this. 'If one day you must catch a witch? And are no Hound to run the wind to exhaustion? Then? Then you must be a sorcerer. One who needs not be a Hound.'" Not-Ellerimo's jaw set firm. "Then it is no witch I hunt, or not yet. It is a sorcerer."

Gewaqsing nodded. "Now there? There I may help. At least, help some. For there are old tales, not tales of Truth, but of days past. And there is a one in those tales. Long ago it was, at least as your kind count days. But that there was a place, it lies where Siknikt finds Sipekne'katik. And the one who walked there and knew much, at least of his kind's knowing. There, perhaps, may lie your Truth young wolf. I cannot find your path, for it is yours to mark and make. But, if you would?

125

Take a gift from me. I am told you know trees. And you will need the coins your kind treasure so. Take this. It will stay with you, and be no burden, in wolf skin or in human." The axe was no hatchet toy, but a true woodsman's tool. It seemed well used, the haft well worn, the head of no metal but rather night-black stone. But the seven point star with a snarling wolf in the center, etched deep in that stone, burned clear to any eye. "And it has an edge it will never lose, one no wood will stay. Not wood, not flesh, nor cold iron either, if such is your need."

Not-Ellerimo turned the axe in his hands. He held it to the chest strap that bore his knife when it was not in the secret place in his thigh, and watched as it shrank, as it clung to the strap. He pulled it from the strap, and watched it grow. He nodded to Gewaqsing. "You honour me, donna saggia. Si. So let it be. My heart-Mother I cannot ask, nor Thiess either. I will seek what I may find of this track you give me, old one." He turned. "And whatever you think me, Katya-wolf, I am wolf enough to hunt. Wolf enough to find!" Then Not-Ellerimo pulled the dagger from his thigh, and set it deep and hard in his chest. A wolf howled, spun, and four swift legs took it to the trees.

* * *

Darek watched the wolf run into the forest. He nodded, and looked at Gewaqsing. "So. It is done."

Gewaqsing shook her head. "Done? No. But his feet step where the Child wished them stepping." She looked to the forest. "E'e, young wolf. You will hunt. But no more than you are hunted." She called to the trees, where she knew more than eyes watched. "Guide him, aye, and guard. He has much to learn and far to go." A wind that did not blow washed and rattled leaves that did not move. Gewaqsing nodded again. "My thanks." She walked to the trees, and was gone.

Chapter 11

Banand-not-i

SIKNIKT, NEW IRELAND – August, 1855

The lighthouse was far behind him. Still wet from crossing the Gaspereau river, the wolf lurked silent in the trees, watching the men set the logging camp. It nodded. Thiess had told him how such things were done, and he saw the words made whole. It nodded again. Tomorrow. No, not tomorrow–the day after. Tomorrow was for trees, learning their tales. A clawed paw pulled the hilt of the dagger from the wolf's chest, and Not-Ellerimo slipped back into the forest. A night in the woods was nothing—but still better in clothes. He took his pack from the bush he had set it behind, and dressed.

* * *

Not-Ellerimo sighed. He had done it so often, he was getting good at it. The blue chalk marks he had found scattered the area, but were more sparse than a camp the size of the one he had seen would, he thought, be happy about. But still, he needed a way to join the camp. Money was one thing, tales and information, those were more than gold. Not-Ellerimo tapped the head of his axe against the tree trunk, his ear pressed tight to the tree. The solid 'thunk' sounded–well, solid. He looked wryly at the knife stuck in its chest strap. He sighed. The mark might not be chalk, but at least it would be... he winced, as something struck his head. He spun on his heel, the axe in hand. The young Mikumwessuk child giggled. She pointed to the ground, to the tied, loose woven bag she had thrown at him. She giggled again, and pointed to the tree, She looked sad, and shook her head. She ran, then came back, a stick of rotten wood in her hand, and pointed at the tree again. The child ran to another, a tall, tall ship-mast pine. She nodded, and pointed to the chalk. Not-Ellerimo shrugged, and swung the bag hard at the ship pine, then swung again, lower down. The red chalk puffed out each time, splodging its signatures on the trunk. Not-Ellerimo swung his axe twice, chopping a wedge low down on the same trunk. He went back to the first tree, and slapped the bag against it, but once only, and cut no wedge. He shrugged. The marks here in this land might not be the same, but it should be clear. He raised his arm, pointed to the trees around them. He waited. The young Mikumwessuk stamped her foot, and jabbed her finger at Not-Ellerimo. He sighed, and wondered if her name was Thiessia. He picked a tree, put his ear against it, and hit it with his axe head. The thunk was, well, less 'thunky'. Not-Ellerimo looked at the young one, and raised the bag. He raised his axe hand, but with one finger pointing in the air. She giggled, and nodded. He sighed again. It would be a long day.

* * *

Not-Ellerimo approached the camp, but did not enter. He took his axe from his belt and held it high. "Ehi! Ehi the camp!"

A logger looked up from the fire he was building. "J'sais pas 'Ehi', mais hello toi! What brings you here?"

Not-Ellerimo shrugged. "What would any man do in the middle of a thousand trees? I seek work, to seek other places with coin in my pocket, and find more women and better birra." He turned, spat into the ground. "Where might I find..."

"The camp Captain?" The man was big, muscles still hard, but older. "Hey, cruiser. You seek work? If you do, I am the one you seek." The man tapped his chest. "Danyel. That is me. What do you do? You cook? You cut? I do not think..."

Not-Ellerimo shrugged. "Io? I find trees."

Danyel laughed. He waved his arms around the camp. "Trees? Oh, indeed they are hard to find here. How can I not hire you?" He shook his head. "I jest. No matter.

130

Our cuts were marked before we came here. We..."

Not-Ellerimo shook his head. "Yes. I have seen them, the marks you speak of." He shook his head again. "I am sure those who came before you were, come dire, most eager to be gone. I... no matter. I will move on. Might I seek a bite and a bed before I go? I have coin."

"Giambionda! Is that you?" The man who turned from the cook fire where he had been stirring the camp pot was old, and Not-Ellerimo could hear the sound of Italy in his voice. "I thought it was you, when I saw you!" The old man turned to the camp Captain. "Danyel, you have known me many years. This I tell you. This is Giambionda! You see his hair? Blonde Gianni they call him! Though not often, not him! Lupo-albero, that is him! Wolf of the trees! He can smell rotten wood a mile away, si, and see a clean cut with his eyes shut! I told you, those fools who marked for us, they knew nothing. For every three trees we cut, two are rotten! Giambi here, he can tell you how to make five, ten, twenty fall and all be worthy of the axe!" The old man turned to Not-Ellerimo, clapped his arms round him. "Good to see you again, old friend!" As he leaned in, he whispered to Not-Ellerimo's ear. "I saw it, your axe. I saw the wolf, though I'll bet no other will. I do not forget the old ways, Benandanti. Call me Calvi." The old man let go of Not-Ellerimo.

Not-Ellerimo stepped back, narrowed his eyes. "Calvi? Is that you? I swear, you are an old oak, you seem to live forever!" He turned to the camp Captain. "I am sorry sir. No matter. I will take my lea..."

Danyel grunted. "Your leave? You will do no such thing. I have known Calvi long. If you are what he says, I am sure we can find you work. But as I spoke. The trees are marked, and..."

Not-Ellerimo smiled, sour as fresh-cut lemon. "Oh, indeed. There are marked trees. Trees you will find not even worth the fire when they fall, and trees missed worth more than the cutting." He smiled, this one bright. "How about a deal?"

"A deal?"

"I saw your... your 'markings'. I made some of my own, not far from here, with clean trails to pull the trunks once fallen. Let it be like this. I will show you three of yours, that when they fall will be rotten through. And you pick any five of mine, and if even one is not all you wish it, then my axe is yours for the taking, and any coin I have with it."

Danyel pursed his lips. "And if you are right?"

Not-Ellerimo shrugged. "Then I can mark more, and you pay me twice what you paid those who came before me, and bed and board also for as long as I stay."

Danyel looked at Calvi. He looked at 'Giambionda'. "I have known Calvi long. Not ever have I known him wrong." He laughed.

"Well, apart from when he thinks he is still a lady's man! No. I will take your deal, Giambi, oui, and hope you are the winner! I will even lend you my own compass to set your path! Silver it is, the silver that does not black. It came all the way from London, so it did. The sawyer in Chipman gave it to me for the fine wood we send him."

Not-Ellerimo's eyes looked over Danyel's shoulder, both miles and many sunrises far away. He remembered Thiess. He shook his head, part denial, part to clear it. "Ah, captain. Do you not remember what Calvi spoke? If lupo-albero I am, when did you ever see a wolf with a lodestone in his paw to find a path?" Not-Ellerimo smiled. "It is indeed a treasure. Keep it close, and I will find your trees still."

Danyel shrugged. "As you wish, strange one. But trees? Yes indeed. Renois! Jacques! Come here!"

* * *

"... and that is why. My Mother, do ye see? So. I hunt them."

Danyel shivered. "The witch, she *ate* her?"

Not-Ellerimo spat. "È vero! Her kind, witches? There is nothing beyond them."

"Nothing? Hard work is, perhaps. Like here." Danyel waved his hand round the camp. The day had been long, long and hot, but at last the sun was setting. "When we do not cut trees, we hunt the wolves."

Not-Ellerimo flinched, but covered it swiftly. "Wolves?"

Danyel nodded. "Aye. So many, there are. There's a tale, though back along it was, of a farmer. He went to trade his grain for meat. An' he was near back to his farm, when they came. Like the hounds of Hell itself, a pack of them, an' they chased him. He beat 'em off with a sled pole, an' threw his meat to the pack. Aye, an' his dog jumped off to chase 'em!"

"Did he die?"

"Die? Not him. He got him home, an' he got his friends, an' they went back for his dog. A strong, brave hound it was. Or so they say, an' they found him, limping sore but breathin'. An' another! Thomas, he was. He got chased near two miles by a pack, an' it took his wife an' their sons to save him! So now we hunt them, aye, and kill them the same. There's good coin in wolf skin. But that's work, an' any wise, wolves is witch kin. So you'll not find one o' your witches here."

Not-Ellerimo raised an eyebrow. "Not here—but other places?"

"Mais oui. There's tell, so there is. Why, up along, at La Coude, there was a family. Il y a cent ans, mais, there was a family there. Young Rebecca, et sa mère Diane. Witches, both. They burned the witch-ling in front of her Mother, and the Mother they hung upside down. C'est vrai! My Father, he told me! And his Father told him!"

"La Coude?"

"Oui. Up along, where the river bends. But best not go hunting there. There's people now, and badges. No, you stay here. You did well, you did. Every tree you marked fell clean! More than I can say for those we found marked when we got here."

* * *

"Calvi! Calvi! Where is he? He is gone, your Giambi. Oui, and coins from the camp stores also!"

The old Italian shook his head. "Lean close, Danyel, and I will tell you." As Danyel leaned close the 'old Italian' blew into his eyes. "Forget, Danyel. There was no Giambi. There was no coin. Forget." The old Italian blew into Danycl's eyes again. Then he went round the sleeping camp, and blew in other eyes. "Forget. Forget..." And an old Italian walked to the woods—but it was a two hundred year old Sorcerer who laughed as he entered them.

135

Chapter 12

Hunter

SIKNIKT, NEW IRELAND – September, 1855

"La Coude? Bah. It's old folks you've been talking to, lad. It used to be La Coude, but it's Moncton now. Aye, they called it after some fuilteach British Colonel, but the fool clerk missed the k, they did. So it's Moncton wi' just a c, an' no k. That's what book learning gets you. You mess up, an' folks think you was right all along. Now Salter's shipyard there wants wood, and all the wood it can get. So we've always got work here. I wish you was stayin'. You're a fine hand wi' an axe, and a finer eye for the right tree to swing it at. But witches? Witches. See, either they ain't real, not nohow, or they is, an' there's not a man's hand wi'out the Church behind it as can stand against 'em. It's a fool's chase you're on, either way laddie."

"Maybe. But still, I must hunt them. My Mother, do ye see?"

"The witch, you say she *ate* her?"

Not-Ellerimo spat. "È vero! Her kind, witches? There is no evil they will not do."

"Evil? Evil is easy. What we do? What we do is long days and ached muscles, and then each day the same again. Yes, there's tales, mind. Aye, the girl you spoke of. Aye, an' older tales too. Back along, they say, there was a mighty Sorcerer down Chignecto way. Or maybe he was just a farmer, like he said he was. Folks say he could blow in your eye and make you dead as dead can be. Mind, there's other folks say it was lies, an' lies on top, 'cos folks owed him money an' didn't want to pay. They had him in court, but he walked free. They say, or there's some as say, he wa' disgusted wi' all of them, an' he wrote down all his magic, an' all his knowing, an' he took them writins to the gates of Hell an' buried them books right there. That's the kind of nonsense folks speak when they don't know cac for true."

Not-Ellerimo nodded, slowly. The gates. Of Hell. Cac, whatever that might be, or maybe solid gold, Hell was no strange land to him, or to any Benandanti. He nodded again. "Hell you say? Well, that's not a place on any map I've ever seen. So I guess those books will never be found."

The logger tilted his head. "Well, likely as you know best laddie. But—well. Your Mother, you say? Maybe..." The logger raised his eyebrows, held out his hand.

Not-Ellerimo sighed, and pulled a coin from his pocket, dropped it in the logger's hand.

"Well. Do ye see, there's a place I've heard of. An' it has a name, so it does. Well, like as it has many names. Places like this one, they do. They say as how, you go there, an' you take a walk, but it's no walk you'll ever come back from. Some, they just call it 'that bloody place'. An' some, they say as how, since the Eel River goes into it, why, then it's Eel Lake, as any know. But there's some–aye, and only some few–as whispers in dark corners, of darker things and deeds, an' they calls it Hell's Gate Lake, they do. If someone was lookin' for, oh, maybe some books wi' maybe some witches in 'em, it's an' interestin' thing, no?"

Not-Ellerimo nodded. Interesting indeed. He dropped another coin into the logger's hand. "Grazie. Still, old tales are old tales. Maybe I'd best seek out the witch family grave. Rebecca, that was her name, yes?"

The logger shrugged. "I know no Rebecca. But I hope you find what you seek laddie. I do indeed."

Not-Ellerimo nodded again. "My thanks. Perhaps what I seek cannot be found. But still. My Mother, do you see?" He turned from the camp fire, walking slowly to the waiting woods.

* * *

The logger watched the flames dance. He waited. The steps were soft, but they came.

138

He didn't turn round—fear took care of that. He nodded to the fire. "I told him, the words you said. I told him!"

"Yes. You did. And I am a man of my word—at least, when it suits my goals. Your wife, she will recover. And this—for your trouble." The coin pouch landed at the logger's side. Hands gripped his head, turning it to look into eyes he would never remember. "I was never here. You found the pouch, and took it to get your wife medicine. Forget. Forget..."

The Sorcerer let go of the logger's head. He stood up from where he had knelt, and looked to the woods. He nodded—and smiled.

* * *

Just beyond the edge of the trees, wolf eyes watched the man let go of the logger's head. The man stood, and looked to the trees. He smiled—and wolf lips pulled back from sharp teeth. The wolf sank back into the trees, and was gone.

139

Chapter 13

Prey

CHIGNECTO ISTHMUS, NEW IRELAND – September, 1856

Not-Ellerimo laid the last wood above the tinder. He took the flint and steel from his pack and set spark to the tinder. Then he sat on one of the two logs he had pulled to the fire. He watched as the flames began to dance in the tinder, to catch the twigs. Soon it would be the branches. Such was the way of a fire. He looked into the fire, but he spoke to the woods. "Must we do this?" He shrugged. "She spoke of here, the elfa. What was it she said? 'Where Siknikt finds Sipekne'katik'. Do you know what that means? I asked, so I did. I asked a child. Though perhaps you saw me even then, no? Siknikt, it is what those who were here long before me, long before you, whoever you are, called New Ireland. 'The drainage place'. And Sipekne'katik, that is 'where the wild potatoes grow'. New Scotland. But I'm sure you know these things." Not-Ellerimo put a branch to the fire, stirring the flames. "Because you went to so much trouble to bring me here."

"Trouble? You do not know the half of it, or not one tenth of that half, brat." He stepped from the woods. "Fear me, child. I have power, and I will…"

"What? You will kill me? Tear my limbs from my body and set them to your soup?" Not-Ellerimo shook his head. He sighed. "Cioè, please. An old Italian who could see my axe, who knew the Benandanti? And then, oh, what magnificent chance, another, who knew of the Mighty Sorcerer and where he once walked? Daverro? If I hunt a trail, and at each choice, one path has fresh meat and the other pisciare, should I suspect nothing? Run blindly to the meat and not think who set it there?" Not-Ellerimo sighed again and shook his head. "Come." He patted the second log. "Come sit. Clearly you have a purpose, and since I am sure there are no books of your knowledge buried deep, you can tell me what I must offer to learn the killing of those who seek me."

The man, not old and not young either, shook his head. "You are—well. Let us say, not what I expected." He sat on the second log, held out his hand. "Jean Campagne. Sorcerer of Beaubassin they called me, though it is no name I ever sought. But still. I am here. And those who called me Sorcerer? And Beaubassin itself? Gone."

"Then the victory is you…"

"Pfah. If you must speak, then speak of what you know, brat. I envy them, both those who spoke and Beaubassin its very self.

Listen, aye, and learn. I was born in la belle France, in the year of no Lord of mine sixteen hundred and forty. Two hundred years old and more, and near all of it in this trou de merde they call New Ireland."

Not-Ellerimo nodded to the fire. "Aye. Thiess was old, and my heart-Mother also. Great power you must have learned."

"Enfant stupide!" Jean's hand lashed out at Not-Ellerimo. And it landed, though not on his face. The point of his dagger sat swiftly in the way.

Not-Ellerimo looked at Campagne. "I am aware I have need of you. But your presence here tells me you have need of me also. Your negotiating skills appear in need of attention." He looked at the point of his dagger, pricked hard against a palm from which no blood flowed. "I say again. Great power serves you, Sorcerer."

The Sorcerer laughed. But the laughter was none of amusement. "Serves *me*? Oh, truly it might seem so. But if one must beware of Greeks bearing gifts, then much more should one stand aside from generous demons." He nodded to the fire. "Your fire is warm. Perhaps a tale might make it warmer?"

* * *

ANGOULÊME, France —
September, 1685

Fifteen years old and feeling ten times that, Jean smoothed the arnica lotion he had stolen over the bruises. That one there from his Mother, for tearing his jerkin. Those two from his Father, for blunting the axe and not sharpening it. And those. Those five, from Père Thomas for knocking over one candle. One candle, and that one not even lit! Jean spat. "Putain! May they all burn in hell!"

"Burn? Oh, Aberystwyth does not burn. Well, unless I set it on fire of course." The voice came from nowhere.

"Wha... what?" Jean span round, but there was nobody there.

"Of course, I mean the real one. Not that ridiculous place Edmund built."

"Who... come out, lâche! Come where I can see you! I will break your bones and..."

The voice giggled. "Break bones? Oh, I prefer to simmer them long and slow. Mostly while the ones they belong to are still screaming. And do stop that turning in circles. You really *don't* want to see me."

Jean spat. "See you? Come out! Come out, and you will see my fist!"

As demons go, the thing that appeared looked reasonably normal. At least, as far as Père Thomas's descriptions had gone, though Jean had always wondered how the far-from-good Père ever knew. Horns? Yes, indeed. Horns. With horns on. More arms on the left than the right? Absolutely. Various sharp pointy things in various hands? Most definitely. Warts, an unusual number of eyes, scales and a tail? All present and most disturbingly correct. Oh. No tail. The demon shrugged–with at least three shoulders. "Will this satisfy you? Or I could do this..." Air shivered, muscles, bones and elements with no true words in any language Jean knew flowed. The middle aged woman shrugged again. With one of the only two shoulders she had. "Well?" 'She' held out her hand. "Scythorax. Demon of the Fourth Circle, Grand Devourer of Munchy Things. Or Lilith. Or 'Stealer of children'." The demon shook her head. "I mean, is that last one fair? I was *hungry*!"

Jean looked at the hand the demon was offering. He looked at the demon. "I see. So I take your hand and–and what? I am your next meal?"

"Oh no." The woman-demon grinned. "Unless you wish it so, of course. No indeed. I heard your words. You have promise. Very little promise, but then your kind are almost always disappointments. But I heard your words. So I make you an offer. Secrets I will teach you, and power I will gift you. I will set death in your eyes, and a fog for memories, and life in your fingers–no small thing for a farmer, true? And there will be more. No living foe will have the power to kill you, nor any dead one. No demon nor god, no beast, no blade, no rock, no iron, nor poison's taste may bring your end."

"I will live forever?"

"Oh, that I cannot say. You see, there must always be the small print."

"Small print? Qu'est-ce que c'est?"

"Oh, it is no thing to worry over. But there must always be a path, do you see? To paint the matter with free will and choice. No. Only one there is who may end you. You alone."

"Moi? I can kill myself? Why would I do that? Ah. Père Thomas has told me of this thing, these bargains made with your kind. You will curse me with eternal pain, or rotting flesh or..."

"Pfah. Père Thomas. Oh, the things I could tell you of... but no matter. No. You will live and have health–such things will be trivial to your talents when you learn what I will teach and offer. Or rather, if you choose to accept that offer. As to why you would end it? That is not for me to say." The demon-woman laughed. "But your kind are weak, yes, and foolish also. If you do..." the air shivered. Fanged jaws laughed. "... if you do end yourself? Then you will be mine forever, and my toy and my feast–over and over, and over more so many times as you scream." Scythorax held out a hand now sprouting claws. "Choose, and swiftly, for I tire of your presence."

* * *

CHIGNECTO ISTHMUS, NEW IRELAND – 1856

145

Jean pulled back his sleeve, turned his arm. The scar was old, wrinkled hard skin. "I tell people it is an old thing from a foolish mistake with a knife when I was young."

Not-Ellerimo shook his head, slowly. "So. For me? A witch. For you, a demon? Is that it? You wish me to kill your demon, and then you will tell me how to kill my witch?"

The Sorcerer raised both eyebrows. "Quoi ? No. Absolutely not. First, because you could not, I think, kill any demon–never mind *that* demon. And second? Because I do not know how you can kill your witch."

"I see. Or rather, I think I do not. For if you cannot tell me what I need to know, it would appear you are useless to me. And if you were useless to me, then I would be useless to you."

The Sorcerer raised one eyebrow. "And?"

"Not 'and', Signore. 'But'. Because, as I am sure you know better than I, both you and, suppongo, the Shadow Girl went to great trouble to set me here before you, and you here before me. You would not do so unle..."

"Unless we were not useless to each other." The Sorcerer of Beaubassin smiled, and nodded. "I could wish I had known you longer. But, for many reasons, that could never have been. You are indeed not what I expected."

"So?"

"Indeed. 'So'. So, it is easy. I wish you to kill me."

Not-Ellerimo's hand whipped to the knife in his thigh. With a speed like lightning he pulled the blade, and slammed it against Jean's throat. A throat that did not resist. A knife that slipped deep in.

And Jean laughed. He laughed, and laughed, laughter that became sad tears. "Do you not remember? What the bitch-demon said? No living foe will have the power to kill me, nor any dead one. No demon nor god, no beast, no blade, no rock, no iron, nor poison's taste may bring my end. But she *said* it! The Shadow Child! She said you could... It was supposed to be... you are... why am I not **dead**?"

Not-Ellerimo shook his head. "Quello? That is no surprise. But anyone may tell a tale by the fire. Me? I sought the truth of yours. For demons, I cannot speak. But that you are beyond what most call human? This I now know. As to your death? Pfah. You are a weak man, Sorcerer. Thiess I knew, and he walked longer than you, and each step was just the step he took before he took one more. And when he died? It was for a purpose he chose. Sì, and my heart-Mother the same. But you? You set your hand to a contract with a demon, and now you seek to run from it."

Jean spat. "Bâtard! If the Shadow Girl had not told me to find you I would..."

"The Shadow Girl. Yes. What of her? Do you know where she is?"

"Wherever it is, I hope she burns, hope she screams! She told me you could kill me!"

Not-Ellerimo's eyes darted in every direction. "Kill you? Oh, I think so, Great-and-not-so-Great Sorcerer. If I understood the words you say the demon spoke, at least. But..."

"Then kill me!"

"Kill you? Because you are bored of living? No. Not ever."

"Then..."

"Then what? *You* will kill *me*?" Not-Ellerimo laughed. "Oh, I think not. Do you see, the demon told you there was no way you could die, save setting death to your own heart yourself, sì? But the Shadow Girl, she told you something other. Enough to make you hunt me, though you could not catch a dead rabbit lying at your feet for the hunt you made of me. So do you know what I think? I think she told you I could give you what you wish. Così, I think she was correct. But there is something I seek also. And you were the one I was told to hunt to gain what I need. And you are here, and I am here, and so I do not need a dead rabbit at my feet to mark my prey found. If I do not get what I seek, you will not get what *you* seek. But do you know what I will do? I will go. And you will not ever find me, for you hunt like a fool in a forest banging a drum to call his prey. No. You will never find me, but I will find *you*, on days I choose. And I will let you see me, and I will laugh, for you will still walk this life you despise. And then I will be gone–until the next time, and the next time, and the next time and the next." And Not-Ellerimo gathered himself and his, and stood, and turned to walk from the fire.

"But... but I do not know."

Not-Ellerimo stopped, turned back. "Know what?"

"I do not know why some witches cannot be killed!"

"Then what use are you to me?"

The Sorcerer smiled. "Because I know who does know. And I know, there is only one who can take you to him, and that one is me. And there is only one path to follow to find him, and that path? That path is my death!" And Jean Campagne, Sorcerer of Beaubassin laughed. He laughed, and he laughed–but the tears that fell from his eyes numbered more than any laughter.

Chapter 14
The road to the Road

SIKNIKT, NEW IRELAND – 1857
"Is it far?"

Jean laid the wood to the fire. The evening was drawing in closer, and the chill with it. "Far, young wolf? All places are far, until you reach them. This place? The Road is everywhere, and nowhere. It is just out of sight, and can never be found. Unless it is your time. It will not be *your* time, but though you doubt me, *some* power I have, some secrets I know. I can take you there. To the Ferryman."

"The Ferryman?"

"Oui. The one who takes those once living to the place they must go."

Not-Ellerimo's eyes went wide. "I know this tale! Charon, of the river Styx!"

Jean raised an eyebrow, shook his head. "Yes indeed, and no. He will not come if he hears you call him by that Roman name. Thieves they were, the Romans." He tilted his head. "Well, Save only Janus. No. Kharon Kharopos, he will come. Though it's Charlie he calls himself now."

"So that is why we seek this place, the lake you spoke of? Because Char... I mean Khar... I mean, your 'Charlie', he needs water for his ferry?"

"No. The lake we will speak of another time. No indeed. He does not captain his ferryboat any more. Indeed, he never did. But that was what the dead expected to see, in those distant times, what their priests had told them. The River, and how it must be crossed, and the fee for crossing. And the Ferryman. It was only a tale, but tales have power. Always, truly, it was the Road, and the passage from what was to, what would come."

"And the fee? If ferries and rivers are just tales that dead eyes see, what of...?"

"The fee? No. The fee is real. And not real also. It is—complicated."

"So what will we do, we two, while we travel this distance that is far, to a destination just out of the sight of any eye?"

Jean smiled, though it was bitter. "Do? What do those such as us always do? One teaches, and another learns. My own power I may not give you, but a Sorcerer I am. I have knowledge, and knowledge is your need."

Not-Ellerimo sighed. Some things, it seemed, never changed. "So I must listen, and you must guide?"

Jean smiled. "While there is always student and always teacher, the student is not always student, and of a time the teacher must learn."

"And so?"

Jean laughed. "As you say, I hunt like a man banging drums in a forest. Might you show me, great teacher, where our supper lies, and how I may cook it, eat it, and such matters?"

* * *

The fire crackled, the two skinned rabbits skewered through on the thin branch Jean was turning over the flames. The fire spat as rabbit juice and fat dripped into it. Jean nodded. "A worthy teaching, young wolf."

The wolf across the flames grinned. A paw reached to its chest, and pulled. The dagger came clear, and Not-Ellerimo licked his lips. "Tomorrow it will be your turn, Sorcerer. But tonight? Tonight, we eat."

* * *

"Forgetting? Pfah. Yes, the demon bitch put it in my eyes. But, truly, it is not beyond any. Without power, yes, it is slower. But still, power is where you find it, grasp it. It is around you, if you reach for it. Sit. No, sit. Close your eyes. For this first time, I will set a circle round you. No, we do not need the eyes of bats, or the gibber torn from an ape's throat, or the smile from a corkindrill. Such

152

nonsense. Well, no. It is not always nonsense. But those are darker paths for other times. Now, sit. Close your eyes. Feel the sun. It is warm, yes? What is that, if not power? It is like the flames of a fire, you say? Yes. It is. But not as you think it. Wood is wood. Flame is–not wood, for sure. Now feel. Now. Normally I would do this with my own life. But, truly, you should not trust me. Take your blade. Set it North, then South. Now cut your wrist. Set the blood-blade East, then West. Now cut your other wrist. Yes, like that. Now let the drops flow onto your closed eyelids. Do not think, feel. Let them flow. Now. Open your eyes. But let the blood flow. There. Do you see it? All round you? It is everything. All there is. It is not those many things you see, it is one thing. One thing that is every other, without, truly, 'other' having meaning. Connected to itself, each self connected to every other. Now. Reach. No, fool boy. Not with your hand. You are part of everything, and everything is part of you. Reach with your you. Feel the wolf, the wolf in the forest. Feel it hunting. It is not wolf, it is you. Feel it–and be it. The prey? It matters not. You are not hungry, wolf-you. You are tired. Sleep. Sleep, and hunt tomorrow. Do you feel it?"

Not-Ellerimo nodded, eyes blood filled and wide.

"Now. Wipe your eyes, and come with me."

* * *

"There. Do you see?"

The wolf lies still, dropped in front of them mid-hunt. It breathes slowly.

"With time, with practice? This could be your path."

* * *

"She taught me much, my heart-Mother. You know of the Dead Man's Hand?"

Jean nodded. "Yes. And it is good you know of it. You will need it. Not all the locks it will set aside are made of iron."

* * *

The Sorcerer shrugged. "Invisibility, you say. Well, it is no easy thing. In fact, truly it cannot be done. You see, you are still there, and light? Well, light does not like things that are there."

"So it is impossible?"

Jean grinned. "To not be there? That is beyond any Sorcerer. But to cheat? That is much easier, though very hard. First you must stop people seeing things. Then you must make them see whatever lies on the other side of the things you do not wish them to see. And if either thing moves, the thing you wish them not to see or the thing you wish them to see where the other lies, well..." Jean shook his head. "It is, truly, enough to make any head ache beyond aching. And it requires a totem of great power, however much knowledge you bear."

"A totem?"

"Aye. A feather from an Angel's wing. Or fresh blooded meat cut from a dragon's beating heart, set in a..."

Not-Ellerimo span round where he sat. "A dragon?"

Jean nodded. "Yes. A dragon. But there are none left living of those. Though the Mikumwessuk talk of..."

"You know them?"

"Dragons? No. I..."

"Not dragons. Though... Well. No matter. But the wood elves. The Mikum..."

"They are not elves. Those are our tales, not theirs. But, oui. I know them. They were this land before we came, and they are still. So. Invisibility? No. Unless you can conjure a dragon. But let us talk of other ways of not being seen. To cast illusion you must..."

* * *

"It is—it is strange."

"What is strange, Sorcerer?"

"Must you call me that?" Jean's eyes were pained.

"Is it not what you are?"

Jean sighed. "If it is what I am, then I suppose it is. I had hoped... but no matter."

"What had you hoped?"

"I... well. Friends? Those I have never had, not truly. And truly beyond truly, not one I could hope would be the one who would kill me, and me feel grateful. Oh, many have wished to kill me, but it was not my wishing made whole. Just their fear, or their hatred, or their desire not to owe what I had given them, or repay me for deeds I had done for them. No I hoped... but no matter."

Not-Ellerimo stared at the flames. "J... Jean?"

"Ye... yes?"

"I hope I kill you. No. I *will* kill you. Even if I do not learn what I need to know, I will kill you Jean. I hope... I cannot do much, but..."

Two faces stared at the fire's flames. And four eyes cried tears neither tried to stop.

* * *

"The Shadow Girl told me of the Benandanti. So 'Calvi' could explain why he spoke for you at the camp. But she told me more. You have been to Hell, yes?"

Not-Ellerimo shrugged. "Yes. It is a thing we do–I mean, did, the Benandanti. Heart-Mother showed me."

"But it is not like the Road that you can find from any place? The priests say Hell and the Devil are always with us, near us. Not, you understand, that I have always been on good terms with priests. But you need a special place, yes?"

"Truly Jean, I do not know. But the Benandanti believed so, so the ways they taught required such places. For Thiess, it was a place he called 'over the water'–a swamp near a somewhere he called Lemburg, in Latvia. When heart-Mother took me, I had to find it myself, to hunt and let it speak to me. Isola della Conna, it was. Yes, a swamp. But a swamp also a river. Or, perhaps a river also a swamp. Così, also 'over the water'. It spoke to me. Swamp or river, it was my..." Not-Ellerimo stopped. Fell silent. "I said it, then. To heart-Mother. I said 'it is my road'. Perhaps...?"

"Your Road? A part of it, yes. But, do ye see, as the logger I cozened into speaking to you said, there is a place. It is North of here, and still no little travel away. It lies in the Mi'gma'ki, where the Eel River flows, near Saint Margarets. They say of it, it is a lake, surrounded by muskeg, what you call swamp. Those fools who walk in there? They do not come back, or come back rarely. And some say, whatever the one who walks out looks like, it is not the one who walked in. And do you know its name?"

Not-Ellerimo nodded. "Si. Your logger, he spoke of it. It is..."

Jean nodded. "Yes. My words he spoke for me, but true ones. Hell's Gate, it is called. Hell's Gate Lake. It is, as you say, swamp. It is, as you say, over water. Do you think it might be...?"

Not-Ellerimo shook his head. "There is no 'might' to it, Jean. And there is this. I may not know the killing of witches. But there is a thing the Benandanti did, that heart-Mother and I did. There are things to be made, and there are ways they must be prepared. But in Hell, I killed witches, even though they lived again. I think it is a place I must go Jean. Thank you my... my friend."

"You know, I said it once, before I truly knew you. I say it again. You are different from what I expected. This I must say. The Shadow Girl, she does not do a single thing without purpose. Her purpose, not yours. And there is always a price that must be paid. I think... I think.. you might..."

Not-Ellerimo smiled. "Do not speak it, Jean. I think she listens at the most convenient—and inconvenient—times. But I believe I know what you would say. And know this. If I am right, about your demon, about what you asked for helping me find what I must know and how I am the one who may deliver it to you? I think, whatever the price, it is less to give than I have already been given."

Chapter 15
Sunset

SIKNIKT, MI'KMA'KI, NEW IRELAND – 1857

The sun was sinking. Not yet down but falling from the sky. Jean pointed. "C'est là."

There was, Not-Ellerimo thought, marsh. He had seen it. And there were, indeed, Marshes. He had seen those too. The—what had Jean called it? 'Muskeg'?—surrounding Hell's Gate Lake were beyond those, as a hill in a farmer's field was set aside by the mountains in which Not-Ellerimo had spent his youth. Indeed, it was only on Jean's word he accepted there was a Lake at all—the muskeg was simply that, as far as his eyes could see. Not taking his eyes from it for one moment, he sat, slowly and carefully. He calmed his mind, his heart, as Jean had taught him, then closed his eyes. He set his knife's blade point to North and South, then each wrist, to East and West, and set his lifeblood to his eyelids, and then to his opened eyes. And he looked, looked truly, with true sight. At what? At nothing, or no thing bound by the world's nature. For each connection, each link from the greater whole to its very self? Each one wrapped tight around the marshes. But where they entered? Slowly, each one faded from view, not one surely bound whatever lay within to what surely lay without. Not-Ellerimo bound rags around the cuts on his wrists, that the bleeding might stop. "Sì. There it is. And, I think, is not, or at least not part of the world about it."

Jean walked to stand beside Not-Ellerimo. He set his arm about Not-Ellerimo's shoulders. "We are here. And I... I have done what I can. It is time, my friend."

"Must it still be, Jean? If I am not what you expected, then you most surely are not what I thought you were when I was told of you. Are there not sunsets you would see, new journeys to make for you?"

Jean smiled, though there were tears in his eyes. "Journeys? I think one awaits me I never thought to be able to make. Kharon, yes, he is the ferryman. But a ferry? It takes you from where you are to some other place you are not. And then? Is that not a journey in and of itself? Who knows. Who knows indeed, save those who have traveled that path already. But whatever that journey, it will be pale compared to this one I never thought to make at all. You are my friend, of a kind I never thought to have. And if I may, I will mark you wrong my friend. For there is one more sunset I would see, oui, and see it with you, that I may take you to the Road, and set you further on your own passage. So let us make our bargain whole, though let us make it no bargain at all, but simply a gift between friends who never knew they would be so, and see that sunset falling even, over this misbegotten blight on the eye."

Not-Ellerimo sighed but nodded. "Come vuole, Jean. Comme tu veux." He shook his head. "Thiess, that grumpy old wolf? My heart-Mother? To find even one of such in a lifetime is, I think, rare. Me? I have three."

The sun sank further.

"So tell me. Was the Shadow Girl lying to me? I think not, for how else can you learn what you must know? But how, then, may the demon's words be set aside? You tried your knife, and..."

Not-Ellerimo shook his head, smiling—even if that smile held salt and lemon both. "Jean, Jean, Jean. Truly, I do not know how you have walked so long and walked in shadow. You tell fables as well as you hunt. I would bet gold bars to copper pennies you know the telling of what I seek. And I would wager diamonds to dust you promised the Shadow Girl not to tell me."

"Wha... what?"

"Oh, Jean." Not-Ellerimo smiled, a true smile. "Did we not speak of journeys? The Shadow Girl? She has her own, that she set us both on our paths so she may reach its end. I think I know what I have been paid for my feet on that path, and it is more than gold or diamonds both."

Jean shrugged, the tears still falling. "Yes. Yes, she came to me, that one. I watched the place that gave me my name burn, and I envied it. Envied, because I could not pass like it was passing. She made me promise not to tell you. But pfah. Fie on her, I say! It is a mystery, yes. But many secrets I have learned. Now, listen close. To kill a witch of the type you seek, it is this way. You..."

Not-Ellerimo's hand clapped over Jean's lips. "No, my friend. Let this wheel turn as she has set it turning. I think we, we two, are not the only dice rolling on this cloth." He took his hand from Jean's mouth.

Jean shook his head. "You are wiser, I think, beyond ten times your years. But, as you say, let the wheel turn. So. How can it be done, this turning?"

Not-Ellerimo pursed his lips. "Tell me."

"Tell you what?"

"What the demon said to you."

Jean spat. "Those words, they are graven in the very diamond you spoke of in my every thought. She said secrets she would teach me, and aye. Secrets I have learned. She said power she would gift, and yes! Power I carry, though it is not the great prize I ever thought it. She spoke of death in my eyes, and I have killed with these same eyes, and a fog for the memories others had that I wished they did not, and life in my fingers. So I have killed, and I have saved, from disease and wound, though not death itself. And then she spoke it, and I thought it glory. That no living foe would have the power to kill me, and…”

“Jean?” Not-Ellerimo smiled, the lemon and salt full back in his lips. “You know my tale. La cagna? I was breathing when she bore me. Then wet rags she stuffed in my mouth, set over my nose, until I breathed no more. A dead thing I am, and none may say it else.”

“But.. bu…”

“Carry on, Jean.”

“She said none dead could kill me either!”

“I know Jean.” Not-Ellerimo smiled. “But I walk. I speak, I talk, I must breathe, and I must eat, and yes, I must do what eating brings a living body to do to set that eating aside. Tell me Jean. Am I dead?” Not-Ellerimo shook his head. “No. I am not dead, nor if those living are those who have not died, I am not living either. Why, it might be said, had the Shadow Girl not set her hand to it, I would not exist! That I do? That, the Shadow Girl made whole. And I saw this, swift and true, when you first spoke. And then you spoke your other words, and so I thought to try them. For demon I do not think I am, and certain sure no god. And my test? For rock, for poison? There was none near. So I set my blade to you, and you lived. Which set your demon bitch’s riddle’s raveling to naught. My blade? It is a thing of power, yes, But it is a thing of metal, and so of no account for her words, your demon. My

163

blade could not kill you. But I know what can, Jean, to set her words aside." Not-Ellerimo held his hands up in front of Jean to see. "And it is better this way, aye, and worse. For it is not in anger, but in sorrow, and not in rage but in tears. And it will not be easy Jean, when these hands are round your throat. Not easy, not for either of us. But yes. I know with all my not-knowing it can be done. And I know, to set the Shadow Girl's feet to where she seeks to be, it is needed. But, and I do not know how I know this Jean, I think there are Rules to such things. And even if there are not, then this here and this now, I will make them. Because it cannot be because the Shadow Girl's Path needs it. It must be your choice and choosing, Jean—only yours."

Jean smiled. Smiled, but on both faces tears were falling. "No, my friend. Not only mine. For you must choose also. And so, I choose. Not just for me, but for my friend also—and still, truly, for me."

"Then let it be so, Jean. For I choose. For me and for my friend, that the paths we have shared continue, and ever will be linked. But I choose something else also."

"And what is that?"

"I choose to watch the sun set."

And the sun fell slowly, each moment of its falling set full of tales. And it fell, and it fell—and it was set. And 'it'?

It was done.

Chapter 16
The Road

THE ROAD

The sun was down. Not-Ellerimo looked down at the body at his feet. "Fare well, my friend."

"Oh, well I fare indeed, but there is no farewell needed–not yet, at least."

Not-Ellerimo span round. The figure was shadowy, but no floating, corpse-shaped sheet. "Je... Jean?"

"Calm, my friend. How could there be a Road to seek, to travel, if not a form to seek it in? Come. It is not easy, but I have the knowing. And I prepared your path in our last roasted rabbit." Jean's specter smiled. "Your part of it, at least." Jean held out his hand. "Come. Come to the Road, my friend."

Not-Ellerimo reached and took Jean's hand. The stars above? Were they the same? The Road about him was–was what? If he looked it left, it seemed some great highway. If he looked right, just one more rutted passage cut wide through New Ireland's forests. If he looked another, it was... Not-Ellerimo flinched. His eyes burned like a thousand fires. He screamed, but his lips were sewn tight, it seemed.

Jean clapped his hand over Not-Ellerimo's eyes. The hand felt flesh, felt real. "No. Not there. We each see what we must, though what we see is but a cloak what lies there wears."

Not-Ellerimo closed his eyes. He waited, then opened them. Above them were stars, stars he somehow knew would never move or turn in the sky's wheel no matter how long he looked. The Road was...

"It's a bloody road is all. Gets all full of its self and pulls a capital out of its butt, but it ain't nothin'. Just a Road. Bugger. It's got me doin' it."

He was old, if old had any meaning for how old he was. But not old like old ones Not-Ellerimo had known. Perhaps old like the elf-woman of the trees, or old like...

"Like rocks? Like mountains? I've seen 'em, I 'ave. From when they wasn't there at all, to when they was gone and gone, and three times gone."

He stood by—by what? Again, it seemed if Not-Ellerimo looked left, it was a cart, a long wagon. Four huge wheels and—thrice he looked—eight black horses. Though never a cart had Not-Ellerimo seen with horses lacking heads.

The old one laughed. "Well, it's New Ireland we're in. If it's good enough for the Dullahan, it's good enough for your eyes it seems. Me, the days can't pass swift enough.

Eighteen wheels beats four any year's passin'." The old one's brows furrowed, and he counted on his fingers. "Well, any hundred an' fifty years, I guess." He slung a great steel-headed hammer over his shoulder. "Now. Him?" He nodded to Jean, "Him, I get. But you? What the bugger are *you* doin' on my bloody Road?" He sniffed Not-Ellerimo. "You ain't dead." He sniffed again. "Hmmm. An' you ain't alive neither."

"Kharon? I..."

The old one swung round pointed a finger at Jean. "I'll get to you later. You got your penny?"

Jean reached into a pocket, pulled out a coin and held it up.

"Right. You get in. I'll be there in..."

Jean shook his head. "Kharon, I... merde. What was it I was supposed to say? Oh. Right. Charlie..."

The old man stiffened, swung his hammer up. "What did you call me?"

"She said to say this: Charlie, it's Dad. He's dead, but I can fix it."

The old man sighed. "Oh. 'She'. Of course. You're them." Charlie looked Not-Ellerimo up and down. "And you are him. Rosie told me about this rubbish. Which is bloody difficult, since I ain't picked her up yet." He sighed, shook his head. "Right. The Shadow told you. Of course she did. And of course he's bloody dead. Again. Bloody Universe is goin' to 'ave a migraine, so it is."

He looked at Not-Ellerimo, then at Jean. "You. Penny. Give it to me."

Jean threw him the coin he carried.

"Now get your butt in the cart. I'll be with you after..." The old one looked Not-Ellerimo up and down. He looked back at Jean. "Well. 'After'." He looked at Not-Ellerimo. "Now you. Talk to me."

* * *

"Bugger." Charlie looked back at the cart. "So. Scythorax. Bloody woman. Or not-woman. I swear, if it's the last thing I do..." His eyes drifted, a million, million forevers away, "... yeah. It probably will be." He shook his head. "And you. Witches. Well, not all of 'em, mind. Look. I don't know what they teaches you in schools these days, but let's start there. Witches. There ain't no good ones, an' there ain't no bad ones."

Not-Ellerimo nodded. "My heart-Mother..."

"Yes. That one. Well, to you, she was one of what they call the good ones, right? But she did bad things too. Or things other people thought was bad. That's all of you, you ones who live and die. Guess what. It's all of us too. Us ones who you don't think die, not ever. But that's another story. Because dyin' ain't... look. It's bloody complicated, that's what dyin' is."

"That's what you do. You take those who die to the place where the dead dwell."

"No. No I bloody don't. I take those who've stepped their last step on what they thought was their road, an' I take them to be Judged, which ain't Judgin', an' I take them to the sunset."

"And then?"

"Then? Buggered if I know. I ain't allowed to go. Anyway. I wouldn't be goin' if I could. There's someone I 'ave to find, an' I ain't found..." Charlie shook his head. "Never mind. That's another story, so it is. Look. Witches. We was talkin' about witches, right?"

Not-Ellerimo nodded. "Yes. Streghe. The Bruxa, when my Mother... I mean, before..." Not-Ellerimo blushed. "I am sorry, old one. Truly, I do not really know. But the Bruxa, she seeks me." Not-Ellerimo's face burned red. "And la cagna? What that one did? The Shadow Girl, she promised me. That I would get my chance to kill her."

"See? Like that. Some folks, they'd say killin', it's always what makes the bad ones bad. Me, I've been there, done that, and kicked whatever I found's butt until it begged for mercy. Then killed it. Am I bad? Are you bad? Is your mo..."

"SHE IS NOT MY MOTHER!" Punching a possibly-god-possibly-not on the jaw might not always be the best plan for long term success. Not-Ellerimo didn't care.

Charlie pursed his lips, smiled. "Hmmmm. That almost hurt. But not quite. So it ain't you. But I knew that. Let me see your hand." The old one took Not-Ellerimo's hand, ran his fingers over broken knuckles. The knuckles clearly thought arguing with the old one was a worse idea than Not-Ellerimo had thought. They healed. The old one nodded. "Right." He coughs. "Ahem. Sorry 'bout that lad. So. No good, no bad, just choices. An' right now, the bloody Dragon, an' no, I ain't tellin' you about them, think they've stopped—well. Everythin'. Includin' me. Which is another long bloody story. So. Right. Now I see what Maya's up to."

"Maya?"

"Hmmm. Forget I said that. Since she doesn't exist yet."

"The Shadow Girl? But I've *seen* her!"

"Yeah. Her an' her Dad, they're like that. Me too, I guess. Anyway. Witches. The one you're after. You, you—what was it? Benandanti? You Benandanti. You go to Hell, an' you kill witches, right?"

"Yes. Or no. You see, we go to gather the harvest, so we kill them, but they don't really die, and..."

The old one sighed. "Yeah. I get it. Persephone meets the Wizard of Oz. Well, 'seph got taken care of. Or she *will* get taken care of." Charlie spat, shook his head. "Bloody Shadows. Time is... well, never mind. Just you know. When I bloody take care of somethin', I don't mess around. But as to your wicked witch of the whatever direction you like? Yeah. You go to Hell. An' you kill 'em. So why don't they die?"

"They're witches! And…"

"They don't bloody die because you don't bloody kill 'em!"

"No, because then we…"

"No. Not because 'then you'. Not because of the harvest. Not because of no next-year-we-do-it-all-again. Because they're smart, that's why. Or at least, they think they are. Look. See this?" He holds up the coin Jean had given him.

"Yes. It is… it was… it is the fare they pay, to have you carry them. The—the dead ones. Jean gave…"

"No it ain't."

Not-Ellerimo didn't say a word. He just looked at the old one. He waited.

The old one raised one eyebrow. "You ain't as dumb as you look. Nope. It ain't no fare. It's a soul." He waved the coin to the figure sitting in the cart. "His soul."

"A soul? But what about…" Not-Ellerimo nodded to Jean as well.

Charlie shrugged. "Yup. That's his soul too. Same thing, two different places. Quando-superstition, that's what Moira calls it. Or destiny-free-will-duality wossname. One of those. Maybe both. That's quando, see?"

A shadow that definitely wasn't there appeared, formed on a wall that wasn't there either. The shadow reached out and an iron rod smacked Charlie on the head. "Quantum Superposition you stupid bloody not-man." The iron rod smacked down on Not-

Ellerimo. "And don't get me bloody started on you, laddie. If it wasn't for the whole fundamental break down in your basic principles of cause and effect, major buggeration to the destiny-free-will-duality wossname and a severe risk of universal ongoing the-hell-with-this-lets-start-all-over-again? Well. I'd kick the bloody Shadows into the middle of never-actually-happened."

Charlie shook his head. "You know you can't do that Moira. Because..."

The iron bar smacked over Charlie's mouth. "Never you mind no because-es Charlie. We don't bloody go there. Just get on with it." And the shadow that had never been there, the wall that had never existed? They were gone.

Charlie shrugged again "Don't mind sis'. She was born triplets. It gets confusin'." He held up the coin. "See, so this is a soul." He nodded to Jean. "His soul. An' that one over there? It goes to be Judged, which ain't really judgin', an' I takes it."

"You take it where?"

Charlie shrugged. He was getting good at it. "Buggered if I know. I ain't allowed to go there. Wherever it thinks it should go, that's my theory. Like, where it should go next. Anyways. That leaves this." He held up the coin. "His soul. Quantum, right? At least, that's what people say, or they will say, when they don't know what it really is. Anyway.

You know how many people there is in what you call the world?"

"No, but..."

"No. Of course you bloody don't. But them people, they keep on makin' more people. An' more, an' more. So where do they come from?"

Not-Ellerimo shook his head. "I am no child, old one. And la cagna was what she was. Men, well, and women, they..."

"No. Not *that*. That's just the smoke an' mirrors they was made with to stop 'em askin' questions. No. If they keep makin' more people, where does the souls come from?"

Not-Ellerimo looked puzzled. He waved his finger, vaguely pointed up.

"No. Not the bloody clouds. They comes like this." And Charlie clenched his hand around Jean's coin. He clenched, and clenched—and fragments of dust began to sparkle from his fingers. "See? Them sparkles, that's soul dust, that is. An' all the little soul dust bits, they wander round, an' they grow. An' sometimes, they bumps into other bits of other souls, an' they join together. An' sometimes, they just grows. Grows 'til—well. 'Til it's big enough. To start over."

Not-Ellerimo watched the sparkles dance, slip from Charlie's fingers. He sighed. "Goodbye Jean. May we meet again, when my..."

"Yeah. About that." Charlie saw the look on Not-Ellerimo's face. "Right. Well, not about that. See, witches. They bloody CHEAT!"

"What?"

"I can't take any deader nowhere, not to Judgin' or nothin', without their soul. Like, all of it. That one..." Charlie nodded to Jean in the cart, "... an' the other one." Charlie waved at the sparkling dots of what used to be a coin. "Bloody witches, some of 'em, they cheats. They cuts a bit out. Like, out of their souls. The ones in their bodies, an' the ones in their coins. Quando-superstition, like. An' they hides it. So since they cuts a bit out, it don't work. Like, I can't send 'em on, can't crush 'em, even if I can get the clipped coin. 'Cos there's the other bit. An' even if it's only a tiny bit, it's bigger than the bits I crushes coins into. So like Copper-knickers said, all the little bits, they go find the bigger bit, an' they joins it again. So the bloody witch, it never bloody dies, even if you kill it."

Not-Ellerimo spat. "So I cannot kill the Bruxa? But I was promised! Still, I will find la cagna. Find her, and..."

"Slow down, laddie. What if you was smarter?"

"What?"

"What if you went to your Hell place, an' you found you your witch, an' you killed her. An' then you took yourself to the Road, to here, an' you found the bloody witch and took her coin. Well, the bit it had. Which is a bugger, right? 'Cos you can't get back here, right? Like, there's, like, this lock-y kind o' magic what keeps livin' folk from gettin' to the Road, do ye see? Like, the lock-y thing, an' the *livin'*?" And Charlie winked. Badly. "Which is a right bugger, see? 'Cos if you could find the other bit, an' you went an' found it? See, there's things I could do with those bits. Well, Heffy could, an'..."

"Heffy?"

"Don't you never mind about no Heffy. There's things Heffy can do, an' that penny would be one of 'em when you can get it, an' you wouldn't be needin' to worry about no witch no more."

"So... so how do I find them, old one? The witch, and the place she has hidden her..."

"Her quando-superstition thing?"

"Yes."

Charlie shrugged. "Well, there's a way. See, I can't tell you what it is. It's against the Rules. Still, like Moira said. Fundamental break down in your basic principles of cause and effect, major buggeration to the destiny-free-will-duality wossname and a severe risk of universal ongoing the-hell-with-this-let's-start-all-over-again. It was a right bugger last time, an' we had Jack then. I guess it's your turn. So I guess them Rules can be bent some. See, I'se seen you here before. An' no. You don't remember. You can't. Bloody Universe would have to notice *that*. An' I can't tell you anythin' about it. So I won't, right? Not a word about you. But I was thinkin'. Witches. See, some witches, an' I'm not sayin' any kind in particular, they eats people. Old people, an', like, younger people too. But they don't eat the bodies. Well, like, some of 'em does that too. But other kinds, like, the kind I was randomly thinkin' of, they eats the, well, what you folks call the soul. It ain't that really. It's memories." Charlie scratched his head. "Well, no. It ain't them either. It's, like, both. But tryin' to explain is a bugger. So I won't. But, like I said, these witches, which ain't no witches in particular, they eats souls. Souls like..." Charlie waved at the cart "... well, like those what the ones I pick up gives me I guess. An' they eats 'em, like you not-witch folks eats meat an' such. An' you know what 'appens to things you not-witch folk eat, right? It turns into you, right?" And Charlie winked. Apparently he thought he needed the practice, so he did it again. "Anyway. That ain't nothin' to do with you or what I said about me seein' you before, right?" And he winked again. Badly. "Oh, and I found this lyin' around. Ain't no good to me. Do you want it?" Charlie passed Not-Ellerimo a fragment of something that looked like metal, but very probably wasn't. Not-Ellerimo took it. "Right. Whatever it is, I never gave it to you, an' I don't know where you got it, not ever. Right?" Then Charlie raised his wheel hammer high over his head, brought it crashing down on the Road—and

the Road, and Charlie, Jean and the wagon?
Were gone.

* * *

The sun was down, and the sky fell dark, with stars that spun on their eternal wheel. But far away, in the distance? Lights speared the night. Not-Ellerimo looked down at the body at his feet. "Fare well, my friend." And around him—the air sparkled.

Chapter 17

Lodestone

SIKNIKT, NEW IRELAND – 1858

Not-Ellerimo sat on a log, the fire he had set burning bright. He looked at the fragment Charlie had not-given-him, his fingers turning it over in his palm. Long hours, long nights he had studied with heart-Mother. The finding ritual was clear in his memory. For that which was sought? The matter was simple, if complex. That which had once been a whole? If parted, it was still a part of that whole. Such was the Law. So a hair from a head? Still part of that head, that body–that person. So, simple, no? To find a witch, a hair of that witch's head, si? But then, no simple thing, for to take it, first he must find the witch, and if he had found her, what need of hair? And the same for sneezed rags or blood, or nightsoiled... well. Nightsoiled whatever witches soiled. So it would seem no part of the Bruxa he had to his hand. But if that were the end of the matter, then there would be no matter to end, no? No Shadow Girl, no Kharon, no Thiess, no heart-Mother, no Jean. So many balls set rolling, it would not be without great need and great hope also. Which meant what seemed so certain was not. So what did he have, that great powers had gone to no doubt great trial to set to his hand? He flipped the fragment again. Not-Ellerimo nodded. Of course. He nodded again. Of course. So. First? First, a lodestone. And next? Next was harder, but perhaps not beyond doing. But the lodestone? Aye. No hard thing to steal, not to one who carried Glory's Hand. But then and all, that would mean far travel, to where such things might be found. So what of it? Not-Ellerimo nodded. Aye. What if, indeed. He used a branch to poke the fire, then nodded again. "Come out." Not-Ellerimo did not look up, but his voice was strong. "You choose your moments, Shadow. But this time? This time is one *I* choose. And I think it is one you will make of your choosing also, for I think you watch your plan with close eyes." He did not turn his head, for if he was wrong? Well. There was nothing to see. But if he was not? Then there was no need to turn. "Shall I tell you a tale, Shadow? No true tale, of course. There are Rules, do ye see? And Rules such as those there are, well then. They must never be broken. Unless, perhaps, they must. I think it would take great need for those Rules to be set aside. But since this is a tale, and only a tale, then we need not worry of that need, no?" He waited, but only the wind sighed. He nodded. "Quite so. So, let it be as it should." He gestured to the flames. "We have a fire, and what better for a fire than a tale?" He waited, half smiling, but did not turn. "Should I say it? I have never thought of it, but I think I do now. For tales, do they not so often start the same? 'Once upon a time'? And yet, why so? Why not simply 'once'? For there to be 'a' time, for the tale I mean, it cannot be the only one. For then it would be 'the' time. Is that what you do, Shadow? You choose, that some particular 'a time' becomes 'the time'? Well then. Since this is only a tale, let it be so. Let it be that once upon 'a' time..."

"Not only once."

The voice was soft, but one he knew. Not-Ellerimo shook his head. "No. No words. For nobody is here to speak them, is that not so, Nobody? Only the wind, and a wanderer telling that wind a tale to pass an eve." He waited, smiled. "Even so. Yes. Once, for this is this 'once' and not some other 'once', upon a time? Once upon a time, it happened. What 'it'? I know not, nor care. It was a thing that could not stand, but would not fall. But in that time, there was one who could make it never be. But not by some magery, some wave of her–I mean..." Not-Ellerimo grinned "I mean their, for we who tell the tale cannot know who, so no wave of *their* hand. The thing that had happened? It could not be stopped. It must simply never be. And so, this one we do not know? They needed–let us say, a lever, to roll this mighty rock of Fate. A tool. And..."

"Yes. You are a tool." The voice was sad. It sounded like it had not had much practice caring about, well, anything–but now it was sad. "But not just a too..."

Not-Ellerimo shook his head, his eyes far away. "It does not matter, friend wind. Not for one moment. For if I am wrong, then there is nothing to matter at all. But if I am right? Then if I were no tool, I would be nothing nor ever have been one single breath of being." He shook his head again. "But to our tale. Do ye see, wind? The one who would set Fate's rock to roll, and to a path it had never found before, they needed this tool. And so they took the 'once upon a time' that was, and they took a someone in it. A someone who had no part to play, save one, but someone who could have a new part of new making. One needed for their lever. And they made him, they did. For in the once that was?" Not-Ellerimo shook his head, a tear in one eye. "Well. In that once? He died. Died before he had one breath in him to breathe, his spirit, and this I think is needed for our tale, his spirit eaten by a witch. And so, in this tale, the one with need? They see their chance. For if they craft the matter differently, then the rock they seek to roll may change its course." Both Not-Ellerimo's eyes were wet, but his voice was steady. "Was it just you, friend wind? Or did I... did he..." Not-Ellerimo shrugged. "Was there choice?"

"Yes. I found you–I mean, the one in your tale found the one dead-born. She... I mean, *they,* told... I mean, you, I mean, not really you, but... *fuck it!*"

Not-Ellerimo smiled, his eyes still wet. "No matter, friend wind. No matter. It is just a tale, is it not? But let us say, for this tale, there was choice offered, and choice taken. And I know not what that choice was, nor should I, but I think I may guess. So for our tale, do you see, let us say that it was a choice I would have made were I there. And in this tale, a part of the spirit of the one eaten by the witch? It was taken, freely given, and held for a future purpose. For the one who was eaten, who was dead? He had a path to walk, and he was taken on that path by one who had the taking. And that, I think matters to our tale. For, do ye see, the witch? She had eaten the dead one's spirit. And so, that spirit? It was part of her, as food is part of us all. And that which was once together?" Not-Ellerimo held up the fragment of not-metal. "Well. That which was once together, it is ever together. Such is the Law, yes? And well do I remember what my heart-Mother told me. That a lodestone, bound to a thing part-nature to the thing you seek, may show you the finding of your..." Not-Ellerimo's eyes furrowed, his lips moving as he repeated his words. He shook his head. "Ahem. Well and all. Do ye see, did the one in our tale have a lodestone? Well then. He might find the witch he sought, and then set that witch to her end. And also, and no small also I think, the one in our tale? He would have lived, whatever came after that living, and not died ere ever he drew breath. A fair price, I think, for being a tool to roll a rock." Not-Ellerimo shrugged. "So thus the tale, or all I think I know of it, and thus the thing. Should I seek me a lodestone, friend wind? For I think I know where one may be found." He waited— but the wind said nothing. He turned, but there was nothing to see. He nodded to himself. Si. If not a yes? Then not no either. Let it be so.

* * *

Of course, the camp had moved. That, the wolf thought, was the nature of such things. But a wolf nose was not so easily set at naught. The camp in the cleared space was busy. Danyel pointed here, shouted there, and those in the camp's service lifted, moved, pushed and pulled. The Gaspereau was still not far, as was right and proper for those who would rather fallen, cleaned trees floated their way to be made timber and not took that path pulled by men's sweaty muscles. The wolf sniffed the air. Yes. Soon the sun would set and night come. Tomorrow would be time enough.

* * *

The wolf followed the logger crew, Danyel at their lead, his compass in hand as they mapped the marked trees. The wolf

183

nodded, stepped back, and Not-Ellerimo pulled the dagger from his chest. He took the corpse-candle from his pack, lit it–and time froze. He stepped from the trees and, using a fallen branch so as not to touch Danyel, knocked the compass from Danyel's hand. Back in the trees, he plunged the dagger to his chest, then in as near one move as he could he blew the corpse-candle dark and bounded from the trees, snarling and howling, running among the loggers. Each one of them found discretion closer friend than needless valour, turned and ran, Danyel among them. The wolf let them run. Danyel would think his lodestone lost, and perhaps seek it. Well enough. One last howl–and the wolf was gone.

* * *

Not-Ellerimo turned the compass in his hand. White metal, the silver Danyel had said it was, and no silver-black at all. The case was round, a bar needle set to a pivot under clean glass, a hand painted enamel card beneath it. He turned it over, looked at the back, the engraved RO over a JE. He turned it back over again. The needle spun, steady North. He held the compass in his hand, and set the fragment of not-metal to the glass. The needle shivered, twitching. He frowned. The glass he might break, but then the lodestone might cease true seeking. And how to bind the not-metal to the bar?

"Aye. It's a right bugger, sae it is."

Not-Ellerimo started, span round. Wolf he was not, but he had not thought any could come upon him and him not know. The man was old, tight and cracked skin—but that skin covered muscles few could carry. Not-Ellerimo's hand went to his dagger.

"I widnae dae that laddie." The old man shook his head. "First, I'd have tae tear your arms from you, an' second, the Shadow Child wuid rip my own frae *me*." The old man shook his head. "Well, she'd try. Aye, an' likely I'd no get tae dae the first, for I'd wager she has her eye on us both right now, an' mair than her eye, sae that each o' us dae what must be done."

"Shadow? She is here?" Not-Ellerimo's eyes darted to every shadow of every tree, but saw nothing. Still, he let the dagger stay un-drawn.

"Waylan."

"Way-what?"

"Waylan. It's me bluidy name laddie. An' sae long as things gae as she sees it must, then all our arms will likely stay in their proper place. I see you hae the lodestone. Aye, an' a problem wi' it also, no?"

Not-Ellerimo raised an eyebrow. "And what is a Waylan when it stands in front of me, old man?"

"Old? Aye, I'm bluidy old. Not-really-but-almost-maybe god of Smiths, I am. And a friend to Darek and Katya also." The old man shook his head at the look on Not-

Ellerimo's face. "Ye think the Shadow leaves any single thing tae chance laddie? Not that one. And certain sure not her Father either. Well, mostly. Or he wouldn't be dead, now would he?" The Smith paused. "Though that one's a one, for sure. Maybe he knew what she would dae, aye, an' planned it also."

"Fuck! I bet he did! The bastard! FUCK!" The voice from the forest was not happy. And just a voice. No sign of the Shadow Girl could be seen—but Not-Ellerimo was certain he knew whose voice it was.

"So you are a... a Smith?"

Waylan shook his head. "Nae laddie. I'm no' *a* Smith. Heffy an' his kind aside, I'm *the* bluidy Smith." He held out his hand. "Compass. An' the other thing laddie."

Not-Ellerimo passed both to Waylan. "I see. Though rather, I do not. But if this is the Shadow Girl's will, then so must it be. Can you... well, the not-metal? Can you...?"

"O' course I can. She'd hardly hae had me be here if could not, no?"

"Is your Smithy far?"

The old man laughed. And it was there. There, where no there should be. There with an open door frame into a space set with tools, with a fire bright burning. "Dae ye see, it knaes, ma' Smithy. It knaes where tae be, an' it knaes how tae be found. When it has tae be, I mean. Sae welcome... well. What dae I call ye? Not-Ellerimo sounds... Pfah. Giambi. That sounds better. Greetins, laddie. Now let us be about things. Oh, an' gie me ma' blade. It's got an edge it will never lose, but I'd like tae be sure."

Not-Ellerimo pulled the dagger from its hiding place in his thigh. He pulled his pack from the same pouch. "Your dagger?"

The Smith shrugged. "Yours also, I suppose. But it was ma' hand that made it. I hae—let us call it a history with knives. Or a future—one of those, anyway." He shook his head. "Bluidy Shadows. Aye, and Crà-draoidh too."

"Crà-draoidh?"

"No matter, laddie. No matter. That's a long tale, it is, and no' for telling here. So. Let's be about matters. Dae ye see, this here?" Waylan held up the not-metal. "This, it's no' any thing any Smith's hand could set tae the needle o' your lodestone. But then, I'm no' just any Smith. Ye need this, sae ye do." He held up a hair of something that gleamed like nothing Not-Ellerimo had ever seen before, that shivered and danced in the air. Silver? Yes, but no. White? No, but yes. Both and neither, and light rippled along its length in the Smithy's grey shadows. "Now, before you get bluidy started, like *she* did, no. It's no' bloody mithril! First, because there's no such thing. Silver-steel's jus' palladium, wi' phosphorus, silicon, germanium an', aye, just a wee bit o' silver. An' if I ever find the bastard who stole my bloody recipe for it, he'll wish all I wanted tae do wa' kill 'im. An' second, because e'en if mithril wa' real, this is what it would want tae be when it grew up. Moon silver this is. You seen those nights the moon hides her face? No' a cloud in the sky, an' she gets all eaten up until she's gone an' dark? Well she's makin' this. Moon silver. All the light she'd put down on the land made solid. Ain't nothin' can cut it, ain't nothin' can break it—an' it holds an edge like a man holds his last dyin' breath. There's moon silver in the blade I made for ye. Aye. An' more than that too." The old Smith put the hair on his anvil, raised his hammer and brought it down hard. The hammer bounced, the moon silver not even bruised. The old Smith shrugged. "There's no' any tool can break it, nor any hot or cold either."

Not-Ellerimo said nothing. He waited, one eyebrow still raised.

Waylan grinned. "Aye. She said ye was different." He shook his head. "There's no' a Smith who can use this, there isn't. Well, save Heffy an' his kind. Unless ye knae its secrets. Unless the Lady hae told it tae listen tae ye. Or if ye're a moon-child." He looked at Not-Ellerimo, his eyes piercing. Then he shook his head. "No. Not yet, an' maybe never. Or maybe always. The path is there, but not your feet—not yet." He shook his head again. "No matter. Let us see what we see." He put the compass down on his work bench, let it settle. He marked the direction it pointed. Then his fingers took the hair of moon-silver, and pushed against the compass glass. It didn't break, but his fingers slid inside. He wrapped the moon silver round the compass bar, binding the not-metal fragment to it. Then he pulled his fingers out, and blew on the compass. He set it to the bench–and it span, wildly, never settling. "There. It seeks the Bruxa now, the spirit she ate still inside her, calling it. And why, ye might ask, does it not seek the spirit in you? Well. I'll tell ye. Because you're not that spirit. Not truly. It's like two paintings, as look each the same as the other. But only one o' 'em is the real one. Does that set fear in ye, laddie?"

Not-Ellerimo shrugged. "I am what I am. And only by being what I am will I get what I was promised."

Waylan nodded, slowly. "It's just like them, ye are. The Shadows. They... but no matter. It's no' mine tae judge. But aye. It seeks the Bruxa. But there's two tae seek. The part o' her in Hell, an' the part she hid. The Hell part, it's bigger. Sae the needle will find it mair than the other. An' then, when the bigger part is found? Well. It will point tae the lesser." He handed the compass back to Not-Ellerimo. He looked over Not-Ellerimo's shoulder, behind him. "Shadow Girl! What...?"

Not-Ellerimo span round. But there was nobody there. He turned back–and the Smithy was gone, and Waylan too.

"Heh. Sorry about that, laddie. I could nae resist. An' I hate goodbyes, sae I does." The voice was laughing–but still, a hint of sadness. "When you need a Smith, come seek me. It matters not where—the Smithy will know. May the Lady watch you laddie." And the forest?

The forest waited.

Chapter 18

Hell Not–Hound

SIKNIKT, NEW IRELAND – 1856
The muskeg waited. Not like a welcoming fire. Nor yet like a bear's open mouth, ready to rend. Rather–it waited. As though it felt no need to threaten, or to strike fear. For whatever came to it, that thing, that beast, that person or power? It would pass into the muskeg. And the muskeg would remain. But that which passed it would not ever be the same, even did it live at all. Not-Ellerimo laughed, shook his head. Such philosophy. Thiess would have his hide, heart-Mother would laugh at him. Jean? Who knew. Friend he was, and Not-Ellerimo hoped still was, wherever his Road had taken him. But the muskeg, Not-Ellerimo knew, cared nothing for any of them, or for what they thought. It simply waited, as it had waited three nights now under a moon that bathed the compass Not-Ellerimo had taken, sat with the cold iron rod, thick and heavy and plaited with fennel, he had gathered also. And now the time for waiting was past, even if not ever past for the muskeg.

But to travel to Hell, first Hell must be found. Thiess had been guided by those of his kind who had been guided by others back through many years. Not-Ellerimo had been guided once by heart-Mother. But now? Now he must find his path alone. He took the compass, and set it in his palm. Wildly it whirled on its axis, which, if nothing else, showed the moon had lent him her favour. Still, it served little to aid him. But he remembered what he had seen. So he took his knife, and set it to a wrist, that blood might flow and be set to his eyes so that they may open and see the world beyond the world. And after he had done so, he examined the streams and rivers of life that flowed from each thing and all, to each other thing and every other one. Examined them, but not to see where they were. But rather, to trace where they began to fade, to pass, as they entered the muskeg. And he nodded, for it was there, if not plain to see. Not a pattern, but not a scrambled chaos either. The trace, where fade made space for more fade, and life was set aside. He nodded again, and gathered his needs about him. If good intentions were not his pave-stones to the place he sought, then rather life itself would guide him, by setting him aside.

Of his journey, Not-Ellerimo knew he would never speak. For words were not suited to the path he traveled. To speak of marsh, of swamp and muskeg, would be but the surface skim of the path he followed. As the weave of life faded, what took its place? Nothing the words of the world might paint. Were there sounds? Yes. Were they grunts of bears, or howls of demons? No and yes, yes and no. Both and neither. But he walked that path, and learned its nature. And as he walked, the compass set in his palm slowed and slowed, jerked and jiggled rather than span. Until even that was gone, and he arrived at a place like every other place he had walked already–but not in anyway the same. For the compass stopped. And he knew, for all his running, that he need run *from* no more, but rather run *to*. So he took his blade and he set it again to his flesh, and he set about that, um, 'other' fluid demanded for passage. He gathered them, and waited. For even here, bright moon was needed. He waited for it to rise, and as she set herself to the sky he closed his eyes and set the fluids over them. He waited, letting the Lady of the Wheel bathe his eyelids–then opened them. Opened them, and stepped back, his blade in hand. And the one before him, she giggled. "Bloody hell. You actually got here. You know, Maya? She's almost as sneaky as I am! She chooses *good*!"

Not-Ellerimo raised an eyebrow. "Maya? And what might a Maya be? Or indeed what might you be? Are you witch? Are you demon?"

"Maya? She is the one you call Shadow Child. Though that is just a name, and she has had many, though she does not yet know it. Or will have—one of those. What she is? Many things, as is the other one. And witch? And demon? Yes, I have been called such. Anwi I am, and Nookomis, Sina and Devana, Hecate and Artemis. So many names. But I have always cherished Arianrhod." The woman smiled. "Look up, wolf-child."

Not-Ellerimo looked up. "What do I seek, you of many names?"

The woman shrugged. "That which is not there."

Not-Ellerimo cast his eyes about the sky. And saw. Or rather—did not. He dropped to one knee. "Mi perdoni, Aradia saggia. I..."

The probably-not-woman laughed. "Sweet boy. You are all my child told me you were. And so, I am here. Because the path you seek? It cannot be found."

Not-Ellerimo opened his mouth—then closed it. He raised one eyebrow, and waited.

Arianrhod raised an eyebrow of her own. She nodded, thoughtfully. "Yes. You are indeed not what I might have expected. So I will speak. Tell me, what did the Benandanti do, each night of Saint Lucia? No. Do not. For I will tell you. They traveled to Hell, or so they thought, to seek and rend dark witches, and bring the harvest to the land. And then? Why, then they would do it the next year and the next, and the next and the next. And always there were witches there to rend, and always harvest to gather. So where did these witches come from?"

"Well, they..." Not-Ellerimo paused. "Mi perdoni. I was *told* they died, but rather, and the dark set aside that the harvest might grow." He paused. "But then, the Ferryman, he spoke that a witch of their kind cannot be killed, for they must be killed both in Hell and in the world we know, where they have hidden..."

Arianrhod clapped her hands. "Clever, clever one! You listen! Yes, it is as the one you call Ferryman spoke. When you Benandanti traveled to Hell, it was not the true Hell, but a shadow of that place. And there, you killed shadows of those you call dark witches, to set the dark aside and bring the harvest. But a shadow is not what you seek. You must find the true Hell, and your true Bruxa-foe. And you cannot. For you do not know the path and your blood and your, um, other potions..." Arianrhod grinned, and Not-Ellerimo blushed "... will not take you there." She waited. And Not-Ellerimo waited also, his blushes mixed with focused eyes. Arianrhod nodded. "I see you will serve what is needed well, young wolf. So this I will say. It is as you found with the Benandanti path. Once you have traveled to the true Hell, you may return if you wish. And two things are needed for the first traveling. One you have, to set Hell's locked door aside. The other? The other is more power than you may bear. But that power I have. And I will lend you that power, to serve your need, if you will vow to serve a need of mine when the time comes. Because the Shadow Child…"

Not-Ellerimo nodded. "Yes. She will kill me when her purpose calls." He shrugged. "But without her I would not have drawn a single breath. And all things must die."

Arianrhod nodded. "So it would seem. But not all is as it seems. And there is a price to this travel. For it will take all there is of the witch blood in your blade, and if you set it to your chest, you will not change skin, but you will die. Is this a price you will pay?" She waited, and Not-Ellerimo nodded. "Then come close, young wolf." And Not-Ellerimo went close to the power before him, and that power whispered to his ear, and whispered more. And after that whisper was no more, he smiled. Smiled and smiled–and nodded. "Sarà un onore per me, saggia. Let it be so." Then he took the Hand of Glory from his pack, and lit it. And Arianrhod raised one finger, and the muskeg was no more, and the Lady was no more and the world was no more. And Not-Ellerimo screamed, and bloody scars across his chest and back oozed, gaping wider far than they had before. He screamed–and the true Hell rose round him.

* * *

HELL – EVERYWHERE, AND NOWHERE TOO

Hell. Where the heart is? For some, yes. Where demons chatter, and gibber laughter while they stretch tortured souls on racks and burn them in fire? For others, perhaps. Where hope goes to die, and good intentions of the few fuel bad outcomes for the many? It may be. And each was there, where Not-Ellerimo stood. They came, and never left, even as they flickered into being and were gone. Temptation, terror, trial and torture—and simple, black night set beside burning daylight truth, as borne by those who knew they were righteous, and knew that same righteousness made any deed, however dark, to bright. To none of which Not-Ellerimo paid heed. Flat he held the compass in his hand, and set his eyes to it, though he kept both eye and ear, aye, and nose, alert for what was about him. For it no longer span in mad circles, but set its mark strong and firm in one direction—a direction he followed. And whether he walked leagues and days, or miles and hours, or only some few feet and but moments was all the same. For Hell or no, he came upon the Bruxa. From one eye? A common cottage, with an apple tree and a goat. But the brick chimney set in tight thatch spewed black smoke, and the smell spoke no wood or coal was it burning. And his other eye? No cottage at all, but a great, grinning bear, mouth set wide where the cottage door would lie. But neither eye mattered. For Not-Ellerimo, all that mattered was the fennel wrapped iron bar he bore. A bar he lifted from his shoulder and brought down on both cottage and bear, and neither also, for neither was what the Bruxa was.

And the Bruxa screamed. "You! It is you! You cannot be here, you cannot...!"

But Not-Ellerimo swung his iron rod hard, and harder, and harder still. Each time it hit, it rended some part of the seeming, whether cottage or bear, away. Until all that was left was the one who had hunted him so long. And he raised the bar over her head, and the Bruxa laughed.

"Well and all. You seek my end? We will meet again, foolish one. I ate you once, and I will eat you again. For I cannot die!"

Then Not-Ellerimo brought the bar down on her head as hard as he might—and she fell, motionless. But Not-Ellerimo knew his task was not yet done. He lit the Hand again, and set the mix of blood and—he blushed, even to think of it. Well, and 'and'. And he set the mix to each closed eye. Eyes that opened on a Road, and on stars that never moved. A Road where the Bruxa waited, even as far off, bright lights speared the black night. The Bruxa spat.

"You! Again and ever, you! Do you think cold iron will rend me here? It has no power."

"Cold iron? Aye. Mayhap not. But my hammer is no simple iron." Charlie swung down from the not-a-cart, eighteen wheels and all, his wheel hammer across his shoulders. "So. You're on my Road. You know my fee, witch-breed. Show me."

The Bruxa laughed again. She held out a single coin. A coin clipped, a sliver missing. "Well, Ferryman. Here is all I have. Will it buy me passage? I think not!"

Then Not-Ellerimo swung his iron stave, and knocked the coin from the Bruxa's fingers. Wolf swift, if not wolf form, he leapt, and gathered it. The Bruxa screamed again, and ran at him—but Not-Ellerimo leapt into Charlie's cabin. He looked at Charlie. "I do not live. But then, I am not dead. It seems your ferry does not reject me, no?"

Charlie shrugged. "Aye. So it seems. We'll have words, me an' it, later."

The Bruxa screamed a third time, and leapt to the cabin. But no entry she found. From seeming air, she bounced back, and hit the ground. In the cabin, Not-Ellerimo lit the now much smaller corpse-candle. The Bruxa froze, but Charlie did not. He nodded to the candle in Not-Ellerimo's hand. "Move fast, wolf. You do not wish to be caught in any passage when it is gone. There is a cold in the frozen time more than any Winter you will ever know."

Not-Ellerimo nodded, and brought out his compass again. It span in mad circles. "What...?"

"It is her coin. Set it safe, laddie. Until she finds her other part, or you do."

Not-Ellerimo nodded. He set the coin in the pocket universe within his thigh. The compass needle settled—and pointed. "Then I will seek what remains."

The Bruxa laughed. "Hah! Not before I take it first, brat!"

The sound of Charlie's wheel hammer hitting her was loud, her silence louder.

Charlie shrugged. "I must be getting clumsy in my old age." He winked. "Or quando-superstition, it must be. Like, me hammer was on me shoulder, but it was on 'er head at the same time. Nothin' to do with me, it wasn't. But it won't hold her long. Now, take the coin and keep it close, and let's be 'avin' you, before it's too hard for Moira not to notice any more. Or worse, the Universe."

A shadow that was not there appeared on a wall that did not exist. An iron bar smacked down on Charlie's head. "Other way round, Charlie. I'm much worse than the Universe could ever be. Now get on with it!" The shadow and the wall both remembered they had never existed, and didn't.

Charlie rubbed his head. "She's got a mean wrist on her, that one. But she's right. If you want to stop running for the rest of your life, you'd better find the other bit of her coin. Now, I can't take you there—I mean, wherever it is you 'ave to be..." Charlie winked. He wasn't very good at it. "... but I got pick-ups everywhere. I could..."

"No."

"What?"

Not-Ellerimo shrugged. "No. As in, not yes. So much has been done. So many steps and choices. There is a reason, and that reason must be molto importante, no?" He didn't wait for Charlie to reply. "But, do you see, nobody has told me this reason. So it must also be just as important that I do not know. Or, perhaps, that I am not told. So, no. Do not tell me. I think I know where I must be, and I think I know how to get there. So set me down, Ferryman. Set me down, and I will do my part."

Charlie set his foot to the brakes, and geared down his carriage. He turned to look at Not-Ellerimo. The sometimes jovial, mostly angry Ferryman had no place in the eyes that looked at Not-Ellerimo. "Yes. Yes, it is important. And no, nothing is by chance. But–well, bugger it. You should know, and you should choose."

Not-Ellerimo raised an eyebrow. "Did I not choose once before, old one? When you saw me on your Road, but saw one I have never been?"

"Aye. That one chose. But he chose for him, and you are not him, whatever... whatever you share. You? You have not. The Shadow Child. She will... she has to..."

Not-Ellerimo smiled, if sadly. "Yes. She does. But that is for tomorrow, or tomorrow's tomorrow-tomorrow. So no. Do not tell me. For I choose. And I choose to walk my Road old one, and seek what must be found."

Charlie shook his head. "You're..."

Not-Ellerimo smiled again. "Not what you expected? Si, old one. I hear that often."

Charlie hauled the carriage to a halt. "Then let it be as you choose, laddie. I..."

Not-Ellerimo shrugged, tears in his eyes. "Do not say it, old one. We both know what comes." He rubbed the lump at the base of the thing the Shadow Girl had called a pocket universe on his thigh, where his knife and pack lived when he had not need of them in his hand. "But if any ask, please tell them. Tell them I went where I must because *I* chose, not because any other forced me, or chose for me." He swung down from the carriage, and nodded to Charlie. The carriage started forward, lights spearing the night. And above Not-Ellerimo's head, the stars that never moved wept tears of glittered diamond–and the Road cried.

Chapter 19

There should have been lightning

THE ROAD

The Road wept. And the never-moving stars above cried diamond tears. Which was not to say Not-Ellerimo scurried round, gathering glittered stones from the ground he stood on. First, because the tears that fell were tears he felt, and not tears he touched and used to fill his pockets. But second, because where he knew he must go, and what would come from that going, made even diamonds hold no value. But for a moment, he sat, watching, feeling. So many roads had led him to this one Road. Could it be that he might sit, and sit, and watch Charlie pass as he gathered? But sit, and sit, and simply *be*? All his life he had followed a purpose, even if one he had not known or of his making. Was not that very thing, that *being*, a purpose worthy of any? He laughed, and shook his head. What, more philosophy? Pfah. Every moment of every life was a sum of many choices, and the fewest of them those of the one living that moment. So let this one moment be his, and this choice be his. He reached into his thigh and pulled his pack. He took out the corpse-candle, and set it lit. Thus and so, step one. He took the compass, and set it to the burning finger–a finger much smaller than it had been when heart-Mother had given him that same candle. Would it be enough? He watched the flame, watched it shiver–then bend and point, speak silent guide of the direction that waited. He nodded. If he was wrong, then most like it pointed to some sad and sorry journey's end. If he was right? Well then. Let it be so. Let the thing he chose be the thing that was.

A shadow that did not exist appeared on a wall that was not there. The old crone nodded. "So. It is true. You are..."

Not-Ellerimo smiled. "Not what you expected?"

The old crone reached out, an iron rod in her hand. She tapped him on his head. "Everything is *exactly* what I expected. *Every* everything. That's how it works. How it has always worked. No. I meant it is true. You are right. They are all out there. Every sum of every choice, every destination on every road. Aye, and Road too. But most people don't see it. That where they go, where they end, is the journey and the ending *they* choose. Because all those stories happen, they just choose the one they wish to be in. And other 'them' walk different roads. You? You are one who sees."

Not-Ellerimo raised an eyebrow. "And so you are saying I am right?"

The old crone laughed. "Of course you are right! And of course, you are totally wrong also. That is the way of it, do ye see?"

Not-Ellerimo nodded. "And so. I choose. I choose that Hell is everywhere. And that 'where' is no simple thing of map or place."

The crone said nothing, waited.

"I choose that when I seek it, I will seek release from it, and my candle will guide me."

"Guide you where?"

Not-Ellerimo shrugged. "If I seek my release, then that is where my candle will guide me. That is the lock my candle will unbar."

The crone nodded. "You are sure?"

Not-Ellerimo smiled, though the smile was sad. "Quite certain." He looked round, but there was no crone, no wall. He laughed. "So let it be so, wise one."

An iron bar smacked him on the head, though there was no iron bar there to do so. "I aten't bloody wise. I'm just always right. And you're bloody lucky Arianrhod is feeling in a good mood, or this wouldn't work however much you bloody chose."

Not-Ellerimo laughed again. "Have it your way, bisnonna."

The iron rod smacked him on the head again. "I always bloody do." And the Road? The Road was silent.

Not-Ellerimo nodded, rubbed his bruised head. He took the blood and, well, not-blood salve and rubbed it over his closed eyes. Of course, Hell rose round him. Which mattered not, because it was not Hell he sought. He set his eyes to the bent candle flame, and his mind to the destination he chose it to lead to. The walls of Hell clung tight. Was it the candle's smaller size? Or was it simply that Hell was where he was supposed to be? He set his mind, and chose the former. He walked, pushed, clawed and struggled his way through the ever more cloying grasp round him. Until it was gone. Until he was free. Until he was there. There, where if there should have been thunder, there was not. There, where if there should have been lightning, none fired the skies. There, where portents, comets and demons of fire, with or without skeletal horses, were most evident by their absence. But there, on a hill by a lone oak tree, where a figure Not-Ellerimo now knew well climbed that very hill.

* * *

FRIULI, ITALY – September 19th, 1835
He drew his knife from the pocket universe in his thigh, stepped behind the tree and waited. The girl got to the top, and she looked down at the cottage. And Not-Ellerimo, because some moments deserve to be more than moments, stepped from behind the tree and tapped her on the shoulder. She whirled round, something that

surely was a weapon in her hand. Not-Ellerimo bowed low, then rose. He made sure his knife was visible, and smiled. "Ciao, Momma."

"Mamma! I'm not your fucking Mam-anything! Who the fuck are you, and where did you get that knif..." The girl stopped. She looked at the oak tree, and down at the cottage. She looked at Not-Ellerimo's knife. "Shit. Oh, bloody shit. You're..." Her eyes darted down to the cottage. She looked back at Not-Ellerimo. "How... you can't be here!"

Not-Ellerimo shrugged. "If it is impossible, then very well. I am not here. You are suffering madness." He lifted his knife. "There is no knife, your Father is not dead, or he is and always will be. Is this what you wish?"

"How do you know about Dad?"

Not Ellerimo shrugged, looked left and right, a teasing smile on his face. "I am sorry Momma. You..."

"I AM NOT YOUR BLOODY MOMMA!"

Not-Ellerimo sighed. He pointed down to the cottage. "Did you not bring me into this world Momma?"

The girl looked down at the cottage, back at Not-Ellerimo. "I... well, I mean..." She looked back at the cottage, back at Not-Ellerimo. "FUCK!"

Not-Ellerimo smiled, if a little sadly. "Of course, I cannot ask if you raised me, protected me, guided me all my life to this day. Thiess, heart-Mother, Jean. Because, of course, you have not yet done so. But you will, will you not?"

The girl, the Shadow Child said nothing. But her finger never left the trigger of the weapon pointed at him. Not-Ellerimo waved his hand to the ground. "I have come a long way, further than you yet know, to be here. Shall we sit?" The two sat. They gazed down at the cottage.

Shadow Child shook her head. "It was such a *good* plan. Bloody had to be. It was the only one I could come up with."

Not-Ellerimo raised an eyebrow. "Was?"

Shadow Child waved her hand at the cottage, at Not-Ellerimo. "You. You should be in New Brunswick. Well, New Ireland."

Not-Ellerimo smiled. "Or Siknikt? Which tale should we walk in... Maya? If not Momma, may I call you Maya?"

The Shadow Child shrugged. "Call me whatever you like. Just don't call me late to dinner." She paused. "But yeah. Please. Momma is..." She looked down at the cottage. "Yeah. Maya."

"May I tell you a story Maya? I told you one before, but this one is different."

"Before? You've never... Oh. Wow. So this is how it feels. You already did, but not in my yet, right?" Not-Ellerimo shrugged, said nothing. "Oh. Right. Spoilers." Maya shook her head. "Damn. This is weird. Sure. Tell me a story... I'm sorry. What did you end up being called?"

"Called? Oh, many things. But best if I not tell you." He looked down at the cottage. "My names there? None I would carry, if I have the choice, and that choice I have now. Others? Whatever the day's deed or trial required. But once–yes, once, someone who would become a friend gave me a name. That one is safe. Giambi."

"A friend? What happened to him?" The girl grinned. "Or to her, maybe?"

Not-Ellerimo's eyes were distant, set far away to a muskeg, to hands tight round a throat. "It doesn't matter."

Maya saw his gaze, so far away. "I think it did."

Not-Ellerimo shook his head. "Not to any not there. But–no matter. So Maya. Let me tell you a story. Just a tale, you understand. And, for you, there may come a time when I tell it again, though less full it will be. But you cannot tell me what you have already heard, or that you have already heard it, if not quite as full as I think it now. You understand?"

Maya smiled, but her eyes were sad. "Yeah. I get it. Spoilers."

Not-Ellerimo nodded, his eyes on the distant days. "Si. So I will tell you a tale, Shadow. No true tale, of course. There are Rules, do ye see? And Rules such as those there are, well then. They must never be broken. Unless, perhaps, they must. I think it would take great need for those Rules to be set aside. So. Once upon a time. And yet, why so? Why not simply 'once'? For there to be 'a' time, for the tale I mean, it cannot be the only one. For then it would be 'the' time. That is what you do, is it not Maya? You choose, that some particular 'a time' becomes 'the time'?" Not-Ellerimo waited, but there was no reply. "Even so. Once upon a time, it happened. What 'it'? I know not, not truly. It happened, I know, to your Father. And it was not a thing the very Universe, or the shadow on the wall either..."

"Moira? You know Moira?"

Not-Ellerimo shook his head. "Let it pass, Shadow. It was a thing that could not stand, or all would be ruin. I think he would do the same for you, your Father. Because you? You could make it never be. But not by some magery, some wave of your hand. The thing that had happened? It could not be stopped. It must simply never be. And so you needed—let us say, a lever, to roll this mighty rock of Fate. A tool."

"No! Well, yes. I suppose. But..."

Not-Ellerimo reached sideways, a finger over Maya's lips. He moved his hand, pointed down to the cottage. "No matter. If I were no tool, I would be nothing nor ever have been one single breath of being." He shook his head again. "But to our tale. You, who would set Fate's rock to roll, and to a path it had never found before, you needed this tool. And so you took the 'once upon a time' that was, and you took a someone in it. A someone who had no place beyond their birthing. To those who might hunt the meaning, the doing, of what was to come? Well. The tool we speak of would never exist, never be seen. So you made me. And where once it had died, this tool? Now I lived. And so could be your mystery, your hidden tool to achieve your goal. But you needed some prod to goad me to your will, so you set me on a path of trial and terror, hunted by one I could not slay without the aid you could bring. And you let me think all was of my choosing, and kept silent the price you would set before me when the time had need. And I have followed that path, Shadow. I have found the Bruxa who ate the other me, found her in Hell itself and slain her. But she is a witch, and a dark one. Her ferry-coin she split in two. And I wondered, indeed, where the second part might lie. And then I remembered how she aged when I had wounded the Bruxa, and her power weakened, and when heart-Mother drained the witch's power from her. So I think I know where the second part of the Bruxa's coin may lie. In that bitch down below. And so..."

"And so you will kill her?"

Not-Ellerimo sighed. "Was that it? The price my first me agreed to, that I might bear part of his coin and walk your path?"

Maya shrugged. "Yes."

Not-Ellerimo nodded. "I see. And the manner of the coin? I think you must tell me, because I think you keep your promises Shadow-Maya."

"It is an emerald. An emerald with a fragment of the Bruxa's coin set in it."

"Ah." Not-Ellerimo's fingers brushed his thigh. "I have always wondered what this lump might be. I see. But no matter. Is it buried in her flesh?"

"No. It... she must... well, there are words and rituals. But she must swallow it, and it progresses as all things swallowed progress. More time, of course, but still. So if you seek it, it will take time. But it does not matter. The plan is..."

Not-Ellerimo smiled, if a little sadly. "You think the plan broken? Because I am not in New Ireland, at whatever time your price was to be paid?"

Maya shrugged, and pulled a glowing sheet from her pocket. "December nineteenth, eighteen fifty nine."

"Is that when you kill me, friend Shadow?"

Suddenly the weapon was in her hand again. "Kill you? Why?"

Not-Ellerimo pushed the weapon away. "Pfah. You have gone to too much trouble to create me, that you would kill me now. No, it is simple, I think. If I were a thing that never existed, then it is important to you I do not exist beyond your need. No, do not tell me. I think I am some flurried flag, to distract a seeking eye and let some other thing they might seek seem nothing. I know not what, nor care. You will kill me, or so you intend. But dying? It is no new fate. I have lived, and seen things few have seen. I do not hold it against you. Indeed, I wish you to know I wish to aid you. Thus and so. Set you to your plans, Shadow-Maya, and I will set to mine. You say December, and its nineteenth day, in the year of eighteen and fifty nine?"

"I... yes. But–but you can't kill her! Or your life will..."

Not-Ellerimo smiled. "Yes. If I kill her now, then my life will not be as it must be. Worry not, Maya-friend. It will be as it must."

"Friend? I'm going to kill you, and you call me friend?"

Not-Ellerimo nodded. "It would not be the first of such in my life. Oh. And where?"

Maya looked at the glowing sheet. "Some loggers, it appears. At a place near... Chipman? Near a river. The..."

Not-Ellerimo nodded. "The Gaspereau." He smiled. "Would it surprise you to know I know it?"

Maya shook her head. "I thought I had given up being surprised by anything. Now I'll have to do it all over again." And shadows warped and shifted, shivered–and she was gone.

Not-Ellerimo stood, and looked down on the cottage. Thus and so. Not now, but in time. He had waited long–he could wait more. He turned, and the hill was empty.

Chapter 20

Pay the price

FRIULI, ITALY – December 14th, 1854

Many days had Not-Ellerimo watched the cottage. Had watched as la cagna emptied the nightsoil to the dung pitch without care. And had watched also as she had taken herself to the woods, to a particular clearing, and always on nights the moon was dark. Taken herself there, and drank potions, spoke words, and danced. Taken herself there to do the deed she needed to do, and no dung pile the destination those times. When that deed was done, so many years came swift upon her that the trees themselves might call her 'old one', and from where he was hidden, Not-Ellerimo had nodded. Indeed. And seen the years fall swift away as she swallowed what she had taken from the ground, fallen amid what else had passed from her. Not-Ellerimo would have wagered diamonds to dust that the thing she swallowed glowed green. And tonight? Tonight was to be one of those nights, or at least, Not-Ellerimo knew la cagna had that intent.

Not-Ellerimo waited, waited until la cagna left the cottage. Then he followed her. Until she neared the clearing. Full swift, for the clearing itself might flow with power, Not-Ellerimo came up behind her and laid a thick branch to her head, that she fell unconscious. Then he took her to a tree, and tied her tight, a thick rag bound about her eyes. And then? Then he did the only thing he could. He waited. Waited until she woke, casting foul words and curses at him, and waited more until what nature she had left took its full course. And again, the many, many years came upon her. And Not-Ellerimo stepped from behind the tree, and he sought what he needed to find in the dung she had dropped. Sought it—and found it. He washed it clean in a bucket he had brought. Then he stood before her. "You do not know me, bitch. Nor do you need to. But I know you, and more. I know what you did, those nineteen years past. And I know the one you serve, and what you carry. Benandanti I am, and witches of the kind you serve? We kill them."

La cagna spat. "Pfah. My mistress has felt what you have done. Felt it, aye, and like as not is here! It is you who will die!"

Not-Ellerimo smiled. "Shall we wait then? Wait for the witch to seek me? I think not. Her? Her I have killed already, in Hell itself."

"You fool! She cannot die! She will come, and she will rend you!"

Not-Ellerimo nodded. "For the most part, you would be right. But this? This in my hand?" He held up the emerald. "This is what keeps her from the final death. And I will take it where it will serve its purpose."

White fear set in the cracked and tattered wrinkles of la cagna's face. "Then finish your work! Kill me now, and go your way!"

Not-Ellerimo laughed. "Do you know, when I came here, that is what I thought to do. But now? Now I see you close? I think I will not. Live, live in your body aged beyond years. Live, or set your own blade to your own throat. I think it is worse than any deed I could ever do." And Not-Ellerimo cut the bonds that held la cagna to the tree. And he left her there, a mirror as his parting gift, and heard her screams as he stepped away from a road he chose not to take. And each scream and every scream made his smile more wide. Then he lit the corpse-candle, and set his thought to the lock he wished unbarred. And Hell rose round him.

* * *

HELL – EVERYWHERE, AND NOWHERE TOO

Not-Ellerimo ran. Ran to where? There was no 'where' to run to. Ran from what? Behind him, demons howled. And a lost friend cried his vengeance for what Not-Ellerimo had done. And the skies tore with fire, and soft suns set on his last day ever, and him all that others had made him and their scars deep upon him. And all was real, and none was, for that was Hell–and Not-Ellerimo ran. He hunted, even though there was no spore, no trail to follow. He knew, it was only important that he hunt, that he sought the Smithy. If it thought him worthy it would... and there! A light, and not the fires of Hell, but a burning forge! Not-Ellerimo ran, and the Smithy doorframe stood before him, Waylan at his forge. Not-Ellerimo ran in, and inside there was no Hell, no howl, no tears.

Waylan looked up. "So. Charlie told me you'd be here. And the Smithy chose the here you would be. Dae ye hae it?"

Not-Ellerimo took the clipped coin and the emerald from the place he had set them in his thigh. He held them out. "I have."

Waylan nodded. "Aye. Sae I see. An' there's none save me could set them right, save Heffy an' his kind." He took them, set more wind to the fire. His fingers slid deep into the emerald, and pulled out a fragment of not-metal. He raised his hammer and looked at Not-Ellerimo. Not-Ellerimo nodded, and Waylan's hammer came down. Up and down, down and up, and the metal flowed, and the metal drank red fire and flowed more. Until one coin there was, and that coin whole. Waylan examined it with a seasoned eye. "Aye. That will dae it laddie."

He passed it to Not-Ellerimo. "It's sorry I am. But I cannae take ye tae the Road."

"My thanks, old one. The Road I can find." Not-Ellerimo took the coin and set it safe in his thigh, lit the corpse-candle and stepped again to Hell. He set his mind to where he must seek, and who. And the Road rose round him, under stars that never moved.

*　*　*

THE ROAD
"No!"

Not-Ellerimo laughed. If the Road had no time, then the Road had *all* time, and this was the time he had chosen. The Bruxa was still where he had left her, at the side of the Road itself. And the lights of Charlie's carriage were no distance gone. They stopped, and new lights bathed both Not-Ellerimo and the Bruxa as Charlie returned. "Si, strega. I have it here. Your passage coin. And it is whole. The bitch you bought with years is screaming in a forest, wishing she were dead, and what you set inside her is now whole again."

The carriage slowed to a stop. Charlie stepped down. Not-Ellerimo passed him the coin. Charlie nodded. "Well indeed." He looked at the Bruxa. "Now. I got your penny. Get in the bloody truck." He dropped his wheel hammer from his shoulder, set it to the ground. "Any time you like. So long as it's

218

right…" SLAM. The wheel hammer hit the Road. "… bloody…". SLAM. "NOW." SLAM, SLAM, SLAM.

The Bruxa screamed, but each slam of the hammer seemed to drag her to the truck. She spat at Not-Ellerimo. "You have no right! I ate you!"

Not-Ellerimo laughed. "May your Judgment be suited to your deeds, strega."

Charlie shrugged. He stepped to Not-Ellerimo's side, leaned in. He whispered. "You know, it aren't really, like, *judgin*, right?"

Not-Ellerimo shrugged. "So you have said, old one. But *she* need not know that. What will come, will come. But this moment? This one is mine."

Charlie nodded. "An' so it is, laddie. So what now?"

Not-Ellerimo looked at the truck. "It is a mighty carriage you captain, Ferryman." His fingers rubbed the small lump on his thigh. "But a full penny it costs to make that one last ride. And if I am right, I think…" he pointed to the lump, raised one sad eyebrow "… my purse is empty of such a coin."

Charlie looked at the place Not-Ellerimo's finger pointed–looked at Not-Ellerimo. His eyes too were sad. "There are…"

Not-Ellerimo shrugged. "Si, Ferryman. Rules. There are Rules." He looked up at the stars that never moved. "I will miss these stars. But I have had my chances, to take what I was promised. And I have chosen my road to travel. Farewell, Ferryman. I think we will not meet again."

Charlie shook his head. "She made better than ever she knew, the Shadow Child. Look. Rules? Bugger the Rules. Climb up, laddie. We will see what the sunset brings, and by my truck and hammer both, I'll get you through its passage."

Not-Ellerimo smiled. "No need, old one. I made a promise to Maya, that I would pay her price and set her need at rest. I saw a sunset once, with Jean. Tell me, old one, did *he* find passage?"

Charlie nodded. "Aye, and the Scythorax was screaming that it was so."

Not-Ellerimo smiled. "Then that is well indeed." He nodded to Charlie. "Farewell Ferryman. May the Road rest easy on you, and you rest easy on the Road."

Charlie shook his head. "Easy? Easy is how you know you ain't doin' it right." He nodded to Not-Ellerimo. "But it's clear, you know that more than most I've ever met upon this Road. Farewell, laddie." Charlie got back into his carriage, set it in gear—and the truck's lights speared the night.

Not-Ellerimo watched the truck disappear down the Road. He looked at the stars, at the Road. Alone? He remembered Thiess, remembered heart-Mother. Remembered Jean. No. He was never alone, for each moment he had lived was his and his forever. And each one he had known was his the same. He looked at the corpse-candle, so small, so melted. The light at its tip was mostly sure, but now and then it flickered. He pursed his lips. No time to plan, no time to ponder. Promises were promises, and he would keep his, however far the journey was, and however long or short the sleep that might be that keeping's cost. The compass would not help him, but the place he knew. And if Hell were every where and every when, the date should not be barrier to his travel. He cupped the candle in his hand and thought of Hell—and Hell rose round him.

* * *

HELL – EVERYWHERE, AND NOWHERE TOO

Not-Ellerimo ran.

To where? There was no 'where' to run to, only need. A promise he must keep. The corpse-candle flickered. He focused his mind on the place he sought, the when, that was his need. The candle shifted, flickered more—but the Hell around him shivered, twisted.

Not-Ellerimo ran.

* * *

Not-Ellerimo ran.

The candle was lower now and flickered more. But running was no new thing to one once wolf. Whether to or from did not matter. It was, indeed, the running. As the candle flickered, the walls of Hell closed some part tighter, some growing part colder. Not-Ellerimo listened, and in the distance, he heard it. A river. He turned his path, with only hope to guide him. What if it was not the Gaspereau? He slapped his head. No! That was not the way of it! If he must pass, it would be as he chose, and only as he chose. So no! It was! It was the Gaspereau, for he chose it so!

Not-Ellerimo ran.

* * *

Not-Ellerimo ran.

His steps were slower now, the walls of Hell clinging more tight each step he took. But each step he forced, as the corpse-candle flickered lower. The river ran louder now, and he knew he was close. He glanced at the candle, flesh-fat dripping more each step he took, flame less bright, the Hell-cold setting deeper into his straining legs. No matter. He would keep his promise to the Shadow Child. He CHOSE to keep it, and no flickered flame would set him wrong.

Not-Ellerimo ran.

* * *

NEW BRUNSWICK – near Chipman – December 19, 1858

The loggers came down the trail. They saw it–a body. Dead? No–it moved, if feebly. They gathered. Should they leave him? Chipman was near, but not close. One of the loggers leaned down to the fallen, frozen form, with legs stiff and iced. He shrugged, the Gaspereau was cold indeed this tide. Had he fallen in, and struggled out? He shrugged–stood back up to move away. The body stirred, lips moved. "L'ho..."–a hand reached up to his arm, feeble at first, then strong. "L'ho... promesso."

One of the loggers started. "Italienne! I have heard that! There was one in a camp I worked!" The loggers muttered among themselves–but living was not dead. They lashed a drag-sled from fallen branches, and set The Italian, for that was what they decided to call him, upon it. Chipman it would be. The village could deal with with him–they would have done their part.

* * *

NEW BRUNSWICK – Chipman – December 23, 1858

"But what are we to do with him? His legs, he will never walk I think, so there is no work in him. We do not have so much we can spare it!"

"Quiet, Francois."

"Be still, wife! Men are talking!"

"Be still yourself, and quiet also. And read your bible more often, or you will come

223

home to an empty house. You know the day that comes, and you know there is no word in that book to cast those in need aside. We will feed him.”

“Mirabelle. We cannot.”

“We will feed him, Francois. Now get back to your chatter. I have food to cook.”

* * *

NEW BRUNSWICK – Gagetown – March, 1861

“And that is how he was found, Doctor Peters. But his legs, they have just taken worse each day it seems. And the smell! We thought...”

The Doctor looked at the young man’s legs. “Yes. Yes indeed. Gangrene.” He probed the legs gently. The young man moaned. “I must cut. There is no other path. He will lose both his legs. Or he will die.”

“We... we do not have much. But we gathered...” the man held out his hand. Some few coins, but not many.

Doctor Peters sighed. “Yes, yes. Of course.”

* * *

NEW BRUNSWICK – Gagetown – March, 1861

Both legs were cut above the knee. The sealing melt was set. Doctor Peters ran his fingers over the cold tar. He nodded. Not his best work, but not his worst. He prodded the tar.

The young man flinched, moaned. "Giambi!"

The Doctor nodded. "Gambi. Yes, it is your leg."

"Giambi!"

"Yes, yes. Your leg. Now, where to set you for your recovery? John Hutchinson, I think. He owes me a good deed, and the jail can pay for your tending."

* * *

NEW BRUNSWICK – Chipman – June, 1861

"Francois, you know I have little. I cannot..."

"George. I have done my part, oui, and Michael and Renois also. It is your turn, and that is all. I will not run risk of a cold bed, or Mirabelle's 'looks' again. We will help as we can, but it is your turn."

"Yes, yes. I suppose. Bring me the Italian. I will keep him as long as I may."

* * *

NEW BRUNSWICK – Chipman – June, 1863

"And do you see, we have tried. Truly, we have. But there is only so much we can do. We wondered. We have money–twenty five whole pounds! Perhaps you might... well.

225

Take him." The man's voice stumbled, and he raised a hand. "Not to... well, we do not mean... perhaps to the Italian people in Liverpool? Or... or..."

The man he spoke to sat in shadows. "Or? Or indeed. Do you truly care?"

The man spat. "We have done our part! We have asked the Parish and the County, oui and the Government itself! None aid us, and we have aided this... this..."

The shadowed man shook his head. "This? This what? Is he not even a person to you? Pfah. No matter. Yes. For your twenty five pounds, I will settle this matter to your need."

"And you will take him to Liverpool? Or to Maine?"

The shadowed man smiled, though the smile was not warm. "I will settle the matter to your need."

The man from Chipman nodded. "Qu'il en soit ainsi. He is outside."

The shadowed man nodded. "I know where he is."

***

NEW BRUNSWICK – 1863
Not-Ellerimo looked up at the shadowed man framed against the night sky. "You see? I keep my promises, Shadow Girl."

The shadowed man took the ring from her finger. "Yes. Yes, it seems you do. Why?"

Not-Ellerimo shrugged. "Because if I do not, what was the point in making them? So now, is it? Now I must be no more?"

Maya sighed. "I will take the emerald from your leg. And you will…"

Not-Ellerimo smiled. "I know. There is no Charlie for me. I have no full coin to offer. But may I ask an asking?"

"What? You know what must be. I need you to be—well, to seem to be, another thing. And to seem to be in a way none of those who might question will do so. And so…"

"And so I must end. Not be here."

"Yes."

"But which?"

Maya furrowed her brows. "What?"

"Must I end, or must I not be here?"

Maya shook her head. "Here, some other place, it matters not. The Dragon will find you."

"I do not know your Dragon, though a dragon I have met, and never thought to. But no. They would only find me where they will look. Or so I was told."

"Told? By who?"

"By me, silly." Maya spun round. Of a sudden, the night was darker, the full moon gone from the sky. But the one who stood behind her had no need of it, for she glowed. "Oh. Too bright? I'm sorry.' The probably-not-a-woman raised a finger, and the glow darkened. "Arianrhod. And I know. You are ecstatic to meet me."

Maya raised both eyebrows. "Arianrhod?"

The not-a-woman sighed. "Yes, yes, yes. Arianrhod, Lady of the Silver Wheel, Guardian of the Silent Forest, Anwi, Nookomis, Sina, Devana–blah, blah, blah." The not-a-woman's voice turned ice cold. "What's in a name? A moon goddess, by any other name, could still rip your bloody arms off and feed you to the Void." Her voice sweetened. "And I have a need your Benandanti here might serve, that will serve yours also. What if he was not here? And not here in a way that would never be found?"

Maya shrugged. "I'm listening. But if I can't get Dad to never have been not here, the Universe is going to get more pissed than even a moon goddess can handle."

Arianrhod nodded. "Indeed."

"And it isn't really up to me. He has no..." Maya glanced at Not-Ellerimo. "I'm sorry, but it's true." She looked back at Arianrhod. "He has no true spirit. He will pass to the Void in time."

Arianrhod smiled. "Not necessarily. Katya?"

"Yes, Mother?" The naked girl was all girl, but she morphed and flowed. And a huge wolf opened jaws full of teeth.

Arianrhod nodded to both Not-Ellerimo and Maya. "Do you see, I have a problem. In this 'once upon a time', those who come here hunt wolves to their death. And I..." she nodded to the huge wolf "... hold wolves close to my heart. So I wondered. What if, not now, but in years past, a wolf came among those wolves these 'come from away' fools hunt? And what if that wolf was not like other wolves, but a leader and a wise one, and one who had friends in the forests? Friends here long before those 'come from away'? And what if this new wolf, he guided those he gathered to new homes and new trails? Forests only Mikumwessuk eyes might find, and forests only those the Mikumwessuk welcomed might run? And then, in this day there would be no wolves for these incomers to kill and skin, to vanish from the land, because they would already be gone?"

Maya's eyes opened wide, and bright. "And the Dragon would never see him, for they would never look in a way that might find him! Yes! Yes!" Then her face turned sad. "But still. He would have no spirit to him. And he would...."

Arianrhod smiled. "I think it just might be possible I have thought of that, hmmm? Katya?"

The wolf warped back into naked girl. She smiled. "Human words! They're so—so empty! And wolves? You always get it the wrong way round!" Her hand flashed, and claws sprouted that dug deep into her chest. She pulled and spread her rib cage open. The claws of her other hand tore deep into her beating heart and ripped out a lump of flesh. She jammed it into Not-Ellerimo's mouth.

"Now eat me!" Her hands dropped, her chest sealing and healing as Not-Ellerimo watched. She grabbed hold of his jaws. "You know what they say. Always swallow. So fucking swallow!"

Not-Ellerimo's throat spasmed—and the lump went down. And as it slid down Not-Ellerimo's throat, it happened. His legs, growing and healing."

Maya blinked. She looked at Arianrhod. "Werewolf?"

Katya sighed. "No. Werewolves. Yuck." She grimaced at Not-Ellerimo. "Look, don't you remember? I told you, before. Werewolves are humans who sometimes get lucky enough to be wolves. I'm a wolf. And now you are too. It's just that sometimes we have to suffer being human. But he has wolf spirit now. No need of your humankind." She looked at Not-Ellerimo. "Go on. I know you want to."

Not-Ellerimo grinned. And he focused, and concentrated–and a huge night black wolf stood where he had lain. The air shivered, and he was back.

Arianrhod looked at Maya. "So. About my wolves..."

* * *

NEW BRUNSWICK – 1830
The huge black wolf watched, as the pack chased the farmer's wagon. He saw the dog leap from the cart and nodded. He looked

behind him, at the Mikumwessuk Elder who waited. She nodded too. Yes. This. This was where the trail began. The black wolf howled–and a new 'once upon a time' danced round him.

Epilogue

Sit-rep–Twice upon a time

350 FIFTH AVENUE AND DOWN – Some day

I grab the brush Dad keeps–OK, kept, at least right now–with the chalk, and scrub out the triangle. Mystic triangles, and sigils I already told you I'm not telling you about, are not good things to leave lying around. Like that time–I shiver, which I don't do often. No. Not like that time. We fixed that, Dad and me. And made sure 'that time' never happened. Because that's what we do. And now it isn't we because it's me. Dad's gone, but I'm going to un-gone him. And I know I can do it, because Hauras told me so. Did you catch it? Not 'impossible'. 'Im-poss-i-bull.' Bull, as in shit. Because Hauras knows what we can do. So he told me how to do it. See, what Dad and me do, and 'do' is the only word I'm using, so get used to it, is we change things. Some yesterdays? They shouldn't have happened. So we un-happen them. Like that time Dad had to slug Archduke Ferdinand's driver and take his place, so the Duke could be at the wrong place at the right time. Because if he hadn't been? Things

232

would have been worse. A lot worse. Dad knows. He saw it. Saw the other 'it' happen. We see all of them, the other 'its', Dad and me. And we remember, even when they never happen. So he un-happened it. But the Archduke was real. He existed, so Dad could nudge him. But Hauras, he told me. He said I couldn't nudge anybody. Or rather, he didn't. He said I couldn't nudge anybody *who ever existed*. Which meant, all I needed was somebody who *never* existed. But not somebody local, like, local where Dad got a hollow-point headache. They'd spot that, the Dragon. No. Somebody who never existed, but from somewhere they weren't looking. The where didn't matter, but the never-existing? Hmmm. Words are tricky. Or at least, they are if you're lucky. I nod to myself. Yes, it could work. So I need a patsy. But it has to be the right patsy. What I'm going to do to them will be nasty. So me not doing it has to be nastier.

Hey. Nobody said I was nice. But that's how it is. Some days? The last thing you need is a good guy. Or girl. I head to the file room.

* * *

SIKNIKT

The forest is dark. And it isn't because everything in it is connected. Connected to itself, to everything else. And the strands, the life, glows bright.

I walk.

233

I envy them. I know they are there, I know they watch me. They haven't lost this, this sight. The world I live in, it's gone. Or mostly. For Dad and me? For Charlie? For... my head buzzes with the stories, stories I never knew I knew. I shake it, trying to quiet them again, the stories.

"It is not easy, not even for you, muin?"

She wasn't there. But really? Really, she was always there. Waiting. Waiting for me. Being. Being her.

"I know why you have come. We feel it, here and in all the here-s. It must be mended. You cannot do it alone. But you are not alone. You see the light, e'e? All things, we are not alone. But him. In your tale he is not just important. He is necessary. As both of you are necessary. So. Let us make it as it must be. You will need this. You know the use of its kind, I think?" The old, elfin woman hands me a ring. "And this." The bottle is red in the darkness, red in the light. "Call it s'k'a blood, witch blood, at least in your words. Or call it whatever you wish." She lifts her arm, the cut still healing, one red drop still at the end of it. "You'll need a knife. Seek out Waylan. Yes, we know of your tales. Your Waylan he has the knowing of knives. And a wolf pelt. You know who to seek for that. Set the blood in the knife hilt, that the power he will need will be his. At least, until the blood is gone. And then? Well, 'then' is your tale, not mine." The Mikumwessuk smiles, then looks sad. She

234

leans to me, kisses my forehead–and the
forest is gone.

***

FRIULI, ITALY – September 19th, 1835

I watch the screen. The remote camera I planted in the bitch's cottage shows me everything I need. The self-delivery. What the bitch does next. She heads to the door, and I grab my Leupold BX-4s. I could see them. The placenta. The umbilical cord. Which meant—yes. The bottle. I knew what was in it. Birth blood, mixed with grappa I'd bet would have had to move up town to even know what a bathtub was. Then the woman, she puts down a mess of kindling, and she puts the placenta on it and the umbilical cord. And she dances round the pile widdershins, which is counter to the sun's course, or anti-clockwise if you don't have some of the friends—or the not-friends—I do, muttering something to herself. All of which, if she only knew, was a total waste of time. She dances three times, then she stops, shouts something she probably thought was esoteric, pours the bottle on kindling and co., then throws the burning stick on it. The huge flame leaping up is fairly normal. The bird that swoops down and transforms into a bent over old woman is normal too—but only if you live in my world, and not yours. I wait. I wait while the Bruxa goes in the cottage, and wait until she comes out of the door, and runs off as a rabbit. Because she's got what she came for. And I know I'm right. But it still needs... I grab my bottle, and the smell of Unicorn Horn and Virgin's Tears fills the air.

* * *

THE ROAD
The shadows untwist from round me. I watch the bitch and her witch head to the cottage door. Timing is going to be tight, and Booker T is nowhere to be seen. I wrap the shadows round me and unwrap them. Because it's the Road. A Road with stars above it that never move. I know I don't have long because Charlie will be here soon. The one I need is standing there, by the side of the Road. He's taken the shape of the kid he never got a chance to be. I go to the kid. "Hey." The kid says nothing. He's watching the Road, watching the stars. "I'm sorry."

"Why?" The kid doesn't look at me. He's still watching the stars.

"You didn't deserve it."

The kid shrugs, his eyes on the stars that never move. "Does anybody?"

It's my turn to shrug. "I guess not."

The kid watches the stars.

"Look, what if I... well, what if it could be different?"

"Different?"

So I tell him. Not just the bits, but all of it. The good, the bad and the ugly. Which is easy, because there really isn't any good. He won't remember, not after, but now? Now, he has to know. To decide. To choose.

"So. I get to kill her?"

"Yes, but..."

The kid shrugs. "Fanculo. I get to kill her?"

"Yes."

I see them. The truck's lights, spearing the night. I wonder what he sees, the kid. The eighteen wheeler stops. Charlie gets out. He sees me. "Bugger. It's you. Rosie, she told me you'd be here." He looks at the kid. "Look kid. I cain't pick you up. Your penny, it ain't whole. But this time, it's different. Heffy an' me, we can fix that." He nods at me. "Or she can. Her way. With all that means." He shrugs. "It's your penny."

The kid looks at the stars. They still haven't moved. He looks at me. "It is my choice?"

I shrug, but I'm holding my breath. "Those are the Rules."

The kid spits, again. He looks at Charlie. "Un'altra volta signore." He looks at me again. "I guess I'll be seeing you."

I look at the kid. "You remember, right? What I said? How it's gonna hurt? Like, real bad?"

The kid shrugs. "I have no body now. Do what I am now suffer hurt?"

SLAM. Charlie's wheel hammer swung from nowhere, hit the kid hard. The kid screamed. Charlie leaned on his wheel hammer. "Make a guess, kid." He waved his hand to the truck. Or to whatever the kid saw. "Door's still open."

The kid nods at me. "I get to ki...?"

If the kid had been a Shadow, he'd have been a natural. I nod.

"Then let it be done. Ma rapidamente!"

I pull the sheet of paper with the monogrammed H in the corner from my pack, and the bottle filled with my blood. I put the paper down in the Road. There's no air on the Road. No. I don't know how I breathe there either. But the paper didn't flare red and white lightning. Not until I put the glass bottle on top, smashed my hand down on it, and cried a long, complex name. See, Barbas? That's just for folks who think Fallen Angels–or one at least, who ended up never Fallen because of Dad–go round putting their real names where anyone can find them. And the sky that never changed, the stars that never moved? The sky opened.

The Angel's wings were battered, feathers broken and twisted. Above him the sky warped in a way that hurt any eye that looked. The Angel spat. He looked up. "Sorry, Boss." He looked at us. "You know, breaking through a Paradox Storm is a right bugger." He looked up. Again. "Sorry... oh, never mind. You know all already anyway." He looked at us. "So where is he? Where's Jack? This was a one time thing, right?" He looks at me. "After you killed him, I mean."

Yes. I killed my Dad. Before I knew he was my Dad. It's a long story. No, I'm not going to tell it to you right now.

The Angel sighs. "So. Paradox Storm means Paradox. Means Jack. Means..."

"Means he's dead, Barbas." Charlie's voice is flat, hard. "And she didn't kill him. Thing is, he died. Before the other time he died. Before he un-Fell you. Before..." Charlie looks round. "Well. Before. The Universe is playing nice workin' real hard to stay not-caught-on-yet. But it can't bluff it forever. So. Get your ass in gear, bird-boy." Charlie turns to the kid. "You got your penny?"

The kid looks puzzled. "My penny?"

Charlie shakes his head. "Bloody schools. Don't know what they teach kids these days. Penny. In your pocket. Fare, for me to take you where you go next." He looks at me, then back at the kid. "Or where I would take you, if you didn't choose to go somewhere else."

The kid shrugs. "I have no pocket, sir."

Charlie shakes his head again. "You got what you need. All you 'ave to do is decide to need it."

The kid closes his eyes, his brow furrowed. After a moment, he opens them. The pants are ragged, torn—but they have pockets. He reaches in, takes out a coin. He looks at it, at the missing notch. "It is damaged. Does that mean...?"

Charlie takes the coin. "It means the Universe knows you chose for sure. No backin' out now." He sighs. "Bloody witches." He looks at me. "She ate him?"

I nod. "The first time."

He sighs again. "Bugger. Right. Where's Heffy when I need 'im?" He looks at me, nods to the kid. "He's goin' to need help wi' that. You know. When the time comes."

I nod. "Yeah. I figured Waylan?"

Charlie nods too. "Waylan. Yup, he'll do." He hands the coin to Barbas. "This one's on you bird boy."

Barbas looks at me. I pull the Emerald from my pocket and hand it to him, nod to the kid. Barbas looks at Charlie. Charlie nods. Barbas looks at the kid. The kid nods. Barbas closes his eyes, and digs his nail into the coin. The kid screams, but a fragment of the coin flakes off. Barbas passes it to me. Then Barbas takes the coin, and holds it to his mouth. He opens his mouth, and fire belches out. The coin melts, shivers, then reforms. But it reforms whole, no slice missing. Then the new penny, untouched by any yesterday I'm going to make damn sure never yester-s but just never-s, glows, casting a shadow. The shadow melts into the emerald, like Dad did to me once.

Have you ever heard a scream that never ended, even though it did? Right. It was like that—but worse.

I pick the emerald up off the ground. It glows. The kid takes the real penny, and swings up into Charlie's truck. I look at Barbas, shrug. "You know someone has to do it. There's only Dad." I shrug again. And no. I'm NOT bloody crying. Just Road dust in my eye. "It's an easy job..."

Charlie and Barbas both nod. "Yeah. With no heavy lifting."

I drop the emerald in my pocket, take the bottle. The smell of Unicorn Horn and Virgin's Tears fills the air-that-isn't-air. And…

* * *

RIGA – 1790

The old man, older than any around him know, puts the leather bag to his mouth. I watch his throat flex as he drinks. I unwrap the shadows from round me, and everyone in the room freezes still. The man nods, slowly. "A witch. I suppose it is fitting one such as you would come for me. You know, there was a time I…"

I sit down, pull my e-file from my skirt pocket. "Yes, yes, I know. Clawses and teethses and fur, oh my. Let's see. Thiess of Kaltenbrun, also known as the Livonian Werewolf." I look up. "A little dramatic, don't you think?"

The old man shrugs, but says nothing.

I shrug. "OK. Look, I've got a problem."

The old man shrugs again. "Then I am glad it is yours."

I nod. "Fair enough. I'll go." I stand up. "It's a shame. That means the witch will win, and the child will…"

The old man looks at me. "You know you are an evil bitch?"

243

I shrug. "It's a dirty job, but someone has to do it." I sit down. And I tell him.

Thiess sighs. "Italy? I swear, it is going to be sore paws I have." He nods. "Yes."

I stand up, pull the bottle from my belt. The smell of Unicorn Horn and Virgin's tears fills the air.

* * *

CIVIDALE – 1810

The shadows warp, and I walk from them. The old one-eyed woman looks up from the potion she is mixing. She nods. "Interesting. I had heard of you. And your Father, of course. I thought you legends without truth. But if you are here, then...?"

She's not the only one interested. Me too, because not many have ever heard of us at all. Which means... "OK, Thiess. Get your ass out here." He comes from the old woman's bedroom. I shake my head. "Getting ahead of me?"

He shrugs. "I am the most powerful remaining of my kind. Mostly because I think I am likely the last. You spoke of Friuli. And to speak of Friuli is, to those who know, to speak of Caterina la Guercia. It was not hard."

The old woman laughs, and shakes the potion bottle. "Aye, but you were, Thiess."

I sigh. "I see. OK, here it is. There's..."

The old woman shakes her head. "Yes, yes, yes. There will be a child, who never existed, but is now real, and a Bruxa who... pfah. Thiess told me all you told him. Yes, I will do my part." She shakes her head again. "Now go, Shadow. For old I may be, but not too old." She grins, and tosses the potion bottle to Thiess.

I sigh–and drink my own potion.

* * *

BEAUBASSIN, NEW IRELAND – September, 1750

The man is not young. But still, while years show in his face, his skin's folds and wrinkles, still he is not old. He watches Beaubassin burn. The red from the flames far off, but somehow close, sits deep in his eyes. "I envy you." The words from his lips are a whisper. Me? I don't whisper.

"Not such a bargain now, maybe?

Jean Campagna spins round. Of course, there's nobody there to see–I've got the shadows wrapped tight round me. He waves what might be mystic symbols in the air, or maybe there's just mosquitoes here. "Come out, demon-bitch!"

"Well, that's hardly any way to speak to a lady." I unwrap the shadows, which shouldn't actually be there this early in the evening. I know he's expecting Mom. But it's me. Horns? None at all. A single arm to the left matching the equally single one to the right. And in my hand? No pointy things. But one thing I often use to make my point. "Not that I'm any lady." I see where he's looking. I hold it up. "Glock. Glock 32, 357 Magnum loads. Yes, and it's pink. A girl's gotta keep her standards, right?" I slip it into my thigh holster, under my skirt. If he's blushing, he's hiding it well. "But no good against you, right?" I walk to Jean's side, look down at the fires. "I'm sorry. Mom's a bitch."

"Mom?"

I shrug. "Not really. It's a long story." I look round. "Hasn't happened yet, either." I look down on the flames again. "You know, I can help."

"Help? None may help *me*." Jean spits. "No matter. You would not understand."

"Understand? What's to understand?" I pull my e-file from my skirt pocket. Yes, girls can have pockets. At least, they can when I design them and have a gun to the head of the guy making them. "Let's see. Jean Campagna. Born sixteen forty in Angoulême, recruited by my bitch not-really Mom in sixteen fifty five. Lots of boring crap, then you get here in—in sixteen seventy. Farmer, loan shark, you piss people off, get pissed off, nearly kill some folks... shall I go on, Great Sorcerer of..." I nod down at the fires "... Beaubassin? Must have been great, right? Eternal life, nothing can kill you—we'll get back to that—and everything going your way, right? And then you find out. What a bitch my not-Mom is. Because. You. Are. So. Fucking. BORED!"

"You know nothing, girl! You..."

My hand lashes out, my Glock in it. It smacks across his face. "Shut up. I'm not done. Because you work it out. Can you be rich? Sure. Easy. But rich folks? They get noticed. Remembered. And you? Thing is, you don't die. People notice that kind of thing. Can you run round and mist every memory of every person you ever come across? Sure. You tried that, didn't you? After the trial. Three bloody years, and no Internet or Facebook to track them down with, but you make them forget. Then another town, another place. So there's poor. Nobody remembers *those*, right? Right. But poor sucks. Cold nights are cold, even when they don't kill you. Stealing a meal here, hunting one there, doing odd jobs for a few coins? Yeah. That's *really* living, all right? Damn. Did I break Joe's copyright? I hope not. He was a good guy. Or will be–one of those. Anyway. Where was I? Oh. Right. Living. Forever. Every day the same day. Every night, the same night. And the walls, they start closing in. Papers for this. Papers for that. And you can see it. It will get worse. And. You. Can't. Stop. It. Or rather, you can. All it will take is one knife, one gun, one rope. And you'll still live forever. Tortured, screaming, torn apart for some new soup or roast dinner, only to wake up again and feel your liver and kidneys slowly, painfully growing back. Yeah. I've been told *all* the stories. Mom loves the kitchen, right?"

"I want to die." Jean sighs. "This is no life. But..."

"But the other wouldn't be either, right?"

Jean shivered. "No. Not in any way. Nor would it be death."

"Well. I might have an answer for you. A way to die, and not to give Mom what she wants. What do you know about how to kill a witch?"

"Well, it is no easy thing. You see, they..."

"No. You know nothing. Or that's what you will tell the one I want you to tell, who *really* wants to know. But you do know a way they can find out. For a price. You see. you will say, it's like this..."

Below us, Beaubassin burns. And we talk, its Sorcerer and I. We talk, and he nods. We shake hands–and I take the bottle from my pocket.

* * *

GLEN RANNOCH, SCOTLAND – September 19th, 800

The hammer sound is loud in the Smithy. I walk in. There's no door–it's not a door kind of place. I see him, hammering at the anvil. Waylan. Wayland. Weyland. Wey-tever. Whatever your W of choice, its who I'm looking for. The Smith. The Crafter.

He hammers. Me? I wait.

248

He doesn't look up from his hammering. "Ye didn't hae tae come here. Ma Smithy is where sae ever it needs tae be lassie. Aye, an' when sae ever alsae, the same." He hammers. I wait. He sets the metal aside, puts the hammer and the tools, each in its place. I wait. "Sae. He got his self bloody killed." He looks at me. "Is that 'killed again', or killed for the first time lassie? Time's a bugger, sae it is, an' you Shadows dinnae make it any easier." He shakes his head. "But it wuid be worse wi'oot ye, that it wuid. I'm guessin' it's a knife ye want?"

I shrug. "No. It's a knife I need. Want or not want isn't part of it. If it was want, I'd want not to have to be here."

Waylan smiles, with a sad edge. "Aye. There's that." He holds his hand out. I show him the bottle. "Hmmm. Aye. It can fit in the hilt. But you're goin' tae need somethin' tae hold it."

I hold out my other hand. "Alginate-based hydrogel."

Waylan nods. "Aye. That will do it. Sucks better than a New York hooker. Well, once New York's been invented it will. Or even Old York." He nods. "You'll be needing a wolf pelt." I raise one eyebrow. "Hey. Sort-of-god-of-smiths here. I knaes stuff, sae I does." He goes outside the Smithy, cups his hands, puts them to his mouth and makes a howling sound. He comes back in. Suddenly a bare female arm wraps round my chest, fingers at my throat. Fingers that sprout claws. The claws aren't the problem. The 'suddenly' definitely is. Nobody, I mean *nobody* sneaks up on me.

"Oh, stop playin' Katya. Or she might fight dirty."

A girl's voice laughs. "Fight? *Fight*? Oh, Waylan. You…"

"Hush girl." Waylan's voice is hard. "That's *her*. The Shadow Child."

I turn round. The naked girl is, well, naked. And, apart from her clawed, furred arm and not-really-hand, very girl.

The girl nods. She's not laughing any more. "Oh." Then she grins at me, looks me up and down. "Well, maybe we could still try. Best of three? Waylan won't look."

Waylan raises one eyebrow. "Katya. We need a wolf skin. Might you…?"

Katya sighs. "Spoilsport." She nods. Bones and flesh shiver, and the girl is gone, a huge wolf in her place. The wolf runs from the Smithy. It isn't long before it returns. It drops what it is carrying in its teeth, some torn edges still bloody. Bones and flesh shiver again, and the naked girl kneels to pick the dropped wolf skin up. She looks at me, shrugs. "Wolves mate for life. Eithne forgot—so I reminded her. Darek told me to wait. I guess this was why." She shakes her head. "Mother keeps telling me 'Harry'. I tell her that is not my path, but she never listens. You know Mother."

If almost-sort-of-gods-of-Smiths are allowed to look puzzled, Waylan's face shows it knows how. He shakes his head. "Is Darek near?"

"As near as I need to be."

I look to the Smithy entrance, and it's him. Not tall, not short. Black hair blowing in the wind and a wool scarf tucked into a leather jerkin. Nothing much to look at—until the looker makes the mistake of looking into his eyes. Eyes that should be against the Geneva Convention. Eyes of Mass Distraction. Grey, like the clouds scudding across the sky, but with flecks one moment blue, and another red. Eyes that know how to smile, like they're doing now, but even when they do, they hold pain—like now. Which is fine. Exactly what the files told me. They told me about her as well. Not just Katya. *Her*. But that's not for him to know, not yet. I nod. "Darek. You know, if you rearrange those letters, you get–well. You 'get'. Not really high on the sneaky scale, hmmm? Never mind. "I'm..."

He nods. "Yes. Yes, you are. So. He is dead. Again." He looks round. "But we are still here. So..."

I shrug. "The Universe is playing nice. It's trying really hard not to notice. I've got a plan. And I'm going to need you all for it to work." I show Waylan the fragment Barbas scratched from the never-now kid's coin. "See, there's a witch. And someone who has to find her. Well, there will be. The witch, she ate... look. It's complicated."

Waylan laughs. "If you Shadows are involved, o' course it is."

I tell him what happened. And how it's not going to. I hand Waylan the soul fragment from the kid's penny. "This is... it has..."

Waylan takes it from me, peering at it. "Aye. I can see wa' it is, lassie."

"He won't know where to find the witch, but..."

Waylan purses his lips. "Sae she ate him. The other him, aye?"

"Yes."

Waylan shrugs. "A lodestone then. Wi' this wee bittie o' the him she ate when he was nae him yet, aye?"

"That was my plan. But he won't know how to find you, either."

Waylan nods. "Most folks never do. But those as has to, they do. Ma' Smithy knows where tae be when it has tae be there."

"Thanks Waylan. So. Darek. Katya. There's this lighthouse. Well, there will be. Could you..."

* * *

The Smithy is quiet. I stuff the knife and the wolf pelt in my pack, and take the bottle from my pocket. The smell of Unicorn Horn and Virgin's Tears fills the air...

* * *

FRIULI, ITALY – September 19th, 1835

I wait. I wait while the Bruxa goes in the cottage, and wait until she comes out of the door, and runs off as a rabbit. Because she's got what she came for. I take the dagger and the wolf pelt, and stab the pelt to the oak tree. The cottage waits below—but I don't. I start down the hill.

*　*　*

ECSED CASTLE – another time

"Fewmets. I thought I had something."

"Show me."

The young man passes the file he'd been updating, one of many and many, and many more, all piled on the desks filling the room, clerks reading each of them in detail, to his Supervisor.

"You see? A senior officer's extra-curricular activities in Whitechapel cease. The officer disappears, but his Tag does not trigger. And a mysterious, legless man appears from nowhere on a deserted beach. It looked *just* like His work! I thought..."

The Supervisor reads the pages. "Thought? Past tense? This looks just like what the Countess is looking for. It smells of Jack, yes, and more than smells." He puts his hand on the young man's shoulder. "I'm sorry Edward. Did you manage to...?"

Edward shakes his head. "No. Her Father came home from the fields too soon."

The Supervisor shakes his head. "I'm sorry Edward. But this is... well. You have to show her. If you're lucky, it's really nothing."

"That's what I thought." The young man shivers. "But I was cross-correlating with the area. I found this." He passes a second file to the Supervisor. "You see? Yes, New Scotland. But New Ireland is not too far from there. A logger, found near an icy, freezing river? One easy to fall into? He is found with his legs rotting from the cold, do you see? A doctor cuts the man's legs to save him, seals them in tar. And the 'generous' locals, who tire of caring for him pass him to some ship captain to get rid of? And then a 'mysterious' legless man arrives on a beach? I see no mystery. Baie Sainte Marie? It is a sea captain richer by twenty five pounds, and richer more by a contract he does not have to fulfill. I would say it is nothing. I... I don't really have to show her do I?"

The Supervisor reads the notes, flipping from one file to the other. "No Edward. I really don't think you do. Which is interesting. Some people, the Countess or not, would have run to her straight away, trying to enhance their station. Other people, the Countess being what she is? They would have pushed the file aside, or put it on another desk. You? You did the extra work, went the extra furlong." The Supervisor pats Edward on the shoulder. "I think this desk is too small for you lad. We'll have to find you a bigger one. You'll make a fine Supervisor, that you will!"

I hold the shadows tight round me, and I pull the bottle from my belt.

* * *

BAIE STE MARIE, NEW SCOTLAND – September 8th, 1863

A cold wind blew along the beach. The empty beach. At least until the shadows flex and shiver. I see Dad drop Jack from his shoulder. Prowess is with him. Who's Prowess? It doesn't matter. Well. She matters. But not here. That's another story. Lots of stories. Shape shifting, empathivore concert pianists are like that. But Prowess' smile is as cold as the wind, and then some. She looks at the body on the sand, the tar cold on its chopped legs. "So what do we do, Jack? He's empty now. You going to kill him?" Dad tells her about the Tag. How the Dragon will know if the other one dies. Told her how the Dragon would smell it on Dad if he killed him. Prowess frowns. "But—but he'll be dead anyway, won't he?"

I could see P's lips moving as she tried to work out how a guy who was going to have been dead for a hundred and fifty years wasn't going to be dead when they'd taken him from. And if that sounds confusing, you're right. It is. But that's not how it works. When you Tag someone, the Tag's in their head with them. Say I Tagged you yesterday, at Carnegie Hall, then took you some other time, some other year or day, century or minute. The Tag wouldn't know you were in the Back-Along, at least, Back-Along relative to when I tagged you. Just know a day was gone and you weren't dead. But when you die? The Tag wouldn't know when. Just that it happened so many days after it was set on you. And I'd get a print of every soul near you the moment it happened. Actually, it isn't like that at all. But it's close enough.

Prowess shrugs. "So what do we do, Jack?"

Dad shrugs too. "Can you put anything in him? Anything at all?"

"There's always a bit left. A fragment. A scratch of his soul. So yes. A few words, maybe."

"Well then. Not Jack. Jason. John. Something beginning with J."

Prowess eyes look far away, across a distant horizon of years. "I knew a boy once. Jerome...."

"Where was that, P?"

Prowess smiles, her eyes still distant. "What? Oh. Trieste. But...." Her eyes focus back on the here and now. "But no matter." Her eyes focus on Jack. Not Dad-Jack, the other one, the one with no legs. "There. It's done." They turn to leave—but as they do, Dad looks over Prowess' shoulder. He looks at me, right at me, even though I know he can't see me. Her looks, and he nods—and he bloody does it. He winks. And I know Waylan was right. He did it. He set me up, to fix what he knew he had to do, but was going to turn out messy with a side order of fucked-up. And I should be mad, because he used me, and I should be pissed, because it was his mess and I had to clean it up. But I'm not. I'm bloody smiling, because I know my Dad knows however good he is, and he's the best there is, there's only one person good enough, one person he trusts, to haul his ass out of the can. Me. And I feel it–the smile on my face a million years wide–and I pull the bottle from my belt.

* * *

See, that's what we do, we Shadows. We find the things that are messed up, and we mess them just enough more to make them happen right–mostly before they ever happen at all. Which is why you're reading this. Why I'm here. No, don't turn round. You won't see me anyway. Not yet, at least. But do me a favour? Sit down, put your head between your legs–and kiss your past goodbye.

The End

If you enjoyed
this book -
please leave a
review.
Authors need
reviews. Please help
readers find this author.

Appendix 1
Glossary

More than one language occurs in this book. Mi'kmawi'simk (Mik'maq), Italian, French, Gaeilge. If it is of use, here are translations, by Chapter.

PROLOGUE:
Fewmets: Anglo-Norma English. Animal droppings.

Bassza meg: Hungarian. Fuck me, a vulgar exclamation, not a request.

Fattyú: Hungarian. Bastard.

CHAPTER 1:
grappa: Italian. A brandy, 70-120 US proof, made by distilling the skins, seeds, pulp and stems left over from wine making. In some forms, closer to moonshine than a formal brew.

Puttana: Italian. A vulgar term for a prostitute.

Bruxa: Italian. Witches with the appearance of an old woman, having the ability to assume any shape and size, both animal and vegetable or even of people. They are reputed to consume the flesh and/or spirits of new born babies.

Mikumwessuk: Mi'kmawi'simk. A member of the Mikumwess, little people like sprites or dwarves, said to be about as tall as a man's waist. They are generally benevolent forest spirits but can be dangerous if they are disrespected. Some Maliseet traditions provide the Mikumwesuk with an origin story: they are the descendants of a tiny hero called Mikumwesu, who was the brother and companion of the culture hero Glooskap.

Ciao Mamma: Italian. Hello Mother.

CHAPTER 2:
Moccio: Italian. Snot.

Strega moccioso: Italian. Snotty kid of a witch, witch brat.

Cornetto: Italian. Little horn.

La cagna: Italian. The bitch.

Marmocchio: Italian. Brat.

Auguri per la tua morte: Italian. Happy death day.

CHAPTER 3:
Bocca al lupo: Italian. Literally, mouth of the wolf. Idiomatically it is to wish good luck, like 'break a leg' to actors in English.

Cazzo: Italian. Many meanings, depending on context. In this use, fuck/ shit/ hell.

Merdo/ Merda: Italian. Shit.

Col cavolo: Italian. Literally, not with the cabbage. Idiomatically, used for no way, not a chance.

Tutto ha un prezzo: Italian. Everything has a price.

No importa: Italian. It doesn't matter.

Mescita: Italian. Tavern or wine bar.

ükskõik millal sa soovid: Estonian. Whatever you like/ whatever you wish.

Nõiduma: Estonian. Witches.

kõigel on oma hind: Estonian. Everything has a price.

ruota degli esposti: Italian. Foundling wheel or baby hatch. It refers to a revolving device, often found in orphanages or churches, where abandoned infants could be left anonymously.

Lupo: Italian. Wolf.

lupo mannaro: Italian. Werewolf.

Dio mi salvi: Italian. Lord save me.

Porcheria: Italian. Hogwash/ rubbish.

Kontrolli end: Estonian. Check yourself.

mida perset: Estonian. What the ass.

Dio mio: Italian. Oh my God/ My God.

CHAPTER 4:
Vivere al lupo: Italian. Living like a wolf.

Värdjas: Estonian. Bastard.

CHAPTER 5:
Benandanti: Members of an agrarian visionary tradition in 16th and 17th century Northeastern Italy, particularly in the Friuli region. They believed in the ability to travel out of their bodies while sleeping,

specifically to fight against malevolent sorcerers to ensure good crops for the coming season.

Bastardo: Italian. Bastard.
Schiava: Italian. Slave.
Morto: Italian. Dead.
Vedi: Italian. You see?
Bene: Italian. Approval or agreement.
una perplessità: Italian. A perplexity.
Indovinelli: Italian. Riddles.

CHAPTER 6:
Stregoni: Sorcerers
pisciare: Urine.
Sì: Italian. Yes.
dies canulares: Italian. Dog days.
Prestare attenzione: Pay attention.
Vado a caccia: I'm going hunting.
Vaffanculo: Italian. Fuck off/ go to hell.
Questo non è niente: Italian. This is nothing.
Saccente: Italian. Know-it-all.
Sciocchezze: Italian. Nonsense.
Mano del ponte: Italian. Bridge hand- for a boat - crewman.
Certamente: Italian. Certainly.
Oste: Italian. Host (of an inn).
Signora: Italian. Lady.
Glooskap: Glooscap, also spelled Gluskabe, Kluskap, or Gluskap, is a significant figure in Mi'kmaq (Mi'kmaw) culture and oral traditions. He is a powerful being, often described as a creator figure,

who shaped the landscape and established many of the natural features of Mi'kma'ki (the Mi'kmaq traditional territory).

Mikumwesu: In some Maliseet and Passamaquoddy traditions, Mikumwesu is a monster-slaying dwarf who is the older brother of Glooskap and the progenitor of the race of little people known as Mikumwessuk. Mikumwesu is heroic, good-natured, and loyal; he is noted as being an excellent shot with a bow, and like his brother, has great magical powers.

CHAPTER 7:

Strada dei gabbiani: Road of the gulls/ seagull road.

Amach as mo bhealach: Gaeilge (Irish Gaelic). Out of my way.

Infatti: Italian. Indeed.

Baiocchi: A coin of the Papal States.

Perdonami, Madonna: Forgive me, Madonna.

Le persone stupide sprecano presto il loro denaro: Italian. The fool and his money are soon parted.

Qualunque cosa: Italian. Anything.

E sarebbe un peccato: Italian. And that would be a shame.

An diabhal sin: Gaeilge (Irish Gaelic). That devil/ that evil one.

Amadán: Gaeilge (Irish Gaelic). Fool.

Fuck tú, a mhuc: Gaeilge (Irish Gaelic). Fuck you, you pig.

Draoidheachta: Gaeilge (Irish Gaelic). Witchcraft.

il diavolo: Italian. The devil.

Sciocchezze, damigella: Italian. Nonsense, damsel.

L'nu'k: Mi'kmaw term for "the people," and it refers to the Mi'kmaq people themselves. The singular form is "L'nu".

Athair: Gaeilge (Irish Gaelic). Father.

Seanmháthair: Gaeilge (Irish Gaelic). Grandmother.

Atookwokun: Mi'kmaw. An old story.

Chepĕchealm: Mi'kmaw. A huge horned serpent or dragon, one who lends power to a sorcerer.

Booöin: Mi'kmaw. Someone who holds and can use magic power. A sorcerer.

Noojekĕsĭgŭnodăsĭt: Mi'kmaw. Lead character in the atookwokun 'The Magical Dancing Doll'. The name comes from a profession – sock wringer and dryer.

Tepknuset: Mi'kmaw. Moon, or Grandmother Moon.

Nitap: Mi'kmaw. Friend.

CHAPTER 10:
E'e: Mi'kmaw. Yes.
Moque: Mi'kmaw.. No.
Etugjel: Mi'kmaw. Maybe/ perhaps.
Puowin: Mi'kmaw. Sorceress/ witch.
Metue'g: Mi'kmaw. Difficult/ hard to do.
E così va: Italian. And so it goes.

lucertola grande: Italian. Great lizard.

Puowi-ni\'skw: Mi'kmaw. Witches.

donna saggia: Italian. Wise lady.

Stregoni: Italian. Sorcerer.

Siknikt: Mi'kmaw. The Drainage Area. A term for a part of what became New Brunswick.

Sipekne'katik: Mi'kmaw. The Wild Potato Area. A term for a part of what became New Brunswick.

CHAPTER 11:

Ehi: Italian. A greeting, like hey, or ahoy.

J'sais pas 'Ehi', mais hello toi: French. I do not know ehi, but hello to you.

Io: Italian. I.

Lupo-albero: Italian. Wolf of the trees.

La Coude: French. The Bend – an early name for what was later to be called Moncton.

et sa mère: French. And her Mother.

Il y a cent ans, mais: French. It was a hundred years ago, but...

Fuilteach: Scots Gaelic. Bloody.

CHAPTER 12:

È vero: Italian. It is true.

Cac: Scots Gaelic. Shit.

CHAPTER 13:

Cioè: Italian. I mean.

Daverro: Italian. Really.

Trou de merde: French. Shit hole.
Enfant stupide: French. Stupid child.
Putain: French. Damn.
Lâche: French. Coward.
Qu'est-ce que c'est: French. What is that.
Quoi: French. What.
Suppongo: Italian. I suppose.
Quello: Italian. That.

CHAPTER 14:
Cosi: Italian. A number of possible meanings, in this case, 'So'.

CHAPTER 15:
Mi'kma'ki: Mi'kma'ki or Mi'gma'gi is composed of the traditional and current territories, or country, of the Mi'kmaq people, in what is now Nova Scotia, New Brunswick
Come vuole, Jean. Comme tu veux: Italian and French. As you wish, Jean. As you wish.

CHAPTER 17:
Crà-draoidh: Scots Gaelic. A magic user who uses the blood of the living for power.

CHAPTER 18:
Sarà un onore per me: Italian. It would be an honour for me.

CHAPTER 20:

L'ho promesso: Italian. I promised.
Qu'il en soit ainsi: French. So be it.

SIT-REP 2:
Muin: Mi'kmaw. Bear – a symbol of courage, as a mother protecting her cubs
Un'altra volta: Italian. Another time.

Appendix 2

Jerome – The Nova Scotia legless man

On September 9th, 1863, two boys (or two fishermen – stories vary) were walking down to the beach at Baie Sainte Marie in Nova Scotia. On the beach they found a man who was unable to speak, his legs amputated and sealed in tar, with a bowl of water and a hunk of bread next to him. Some versions of the story say a dark, mysterious ship had been seen the previous day, some say no ship was seen. He was taken in by a local family in Cheticamp, and named Jerome. Some say he never spoke, some say he only ever spoke the name he had been given, Jerome, and sometimes the word 'Trieste'.

The family who took him in genuinely took good care of him. He had his own room, which was no small thing in a family with thirteen children. He lived with the family for forty nine years, dying in 1912. His gravestone can still be seen.

Appendix 3
Thiess of Kaltenbrun

Kaltenbrun was a town in Livonia (the modern Latvia and Lithuania). Thiess of Kaltenbrunn was a Livonian man who was put on trial for heresy in in 1692. In his eighties, Thiess openly said he was a werewolf. He said he would travel to Hell three times a year with other werewolves to fight witches, and return the grain and livestock the witches had stolen back to the world people lived in, and make the harvest return.
7

Appendix 4
Caterina la Guercia – Caterina One Eye

Caterina was a Cividale de Friuli woman who was taken under investigation in 1582, accused of practicing various dark witch arts. Under questioning she said she did indeed know rituals and magics, which she said she used to cure children's sicknesses. She denied being a Benandante but said her dead husband was one and that he used to enter trances, causing his spirit to leave his body and pass among the dead.

Appendix 5

Jean Campagna, the Sorcerer of Beaubassin

In 1670, Sieur Hector de Grandfontaine came to what would become New Brunswick, but was then older names. For France, Acadia. For the First Nations? Other names. He arrived to become Governor, , but he did not come alone. With him on the "Saint Sébastien" was the astronomer Jean Richer, who would acquire fame in science. But also there was another. Jean Campagna, who would become known by a different name, if nearly as famous. The Sorcerer of Beaubassin.

Jean Campagna was born in 1640, in Angoulême, which is north east of Bordeaux and south east of La Rochelle. He came to what would one day become New Brunswick came to Acadia as a hired servant and farmer. After time in other places, he arrived at Beaubassin, which lay on what is now the New Brunswick border with Nova Scotia.

After having been a resident there for some time, the accusations began. People said he had the power of sorcery, and had killed both men and animals. And in 1684, the then Governor of Acadia ordered his arrest. He was detained nearly a year before he was put to trial. Numerous witnesses said he had got into an altercation with one Andrée Martin, widow of François Pellerin, who had beaten him with a stick because of his actions towards a young girl. Campagna, it was said, told her she would be sorry for what she had done. Later, while Campagna was working in the marshes, it was said Campagna blew into her then husband's eye, after which the husband took ill, with pains in his head and fever. The husband later died, a fate witnesses said was clearly of Campagna's doing, and no natural death. Another accusation came from an Irishman who said Campagna had sought to marry the Irishman's daughter. But the Irishman's wife refused, and, it was said, Campagna again said the one who had offended him would suffer. And a little over a week later, a number of the family's cows took ill and were near death. Even a priestly intervention did not cure them. But the Governor heard of the matter, and threatened Campagna with his sword. One day after the Governor's threat, the animals recovered. Despite all the accusations, Campagna was acquitted, though he was told to leave Beaubassin. And of him, little was heard again.

Appendix 6

Point Lepreau Lighthouse – New Brunswick

Point Lepreau is a cape in southwestern New Brunswick, Canada. It is at the southern tip of a 10 km-long peninsula that extends into the Bay of Fundy. This peninsula contains the boundary between Saint John County to the east and Charlotte County to the west, although the southernmost tip at Point Lepreau is within Charlotte County. Point Lepreau forms the eastern limit of Maces Bay.

The Point Lepreau Lighthouse is a historical structure, built in 1831 and has been modified over the years, including a move of the lower light in 1840. The lighthouse is a square, tapered wooden tower with a lantern, and it is painted white with a red horizontal band. It is now a heritage lighthouse, valued for its historical and architectural significance.

Appendix 7

Hells Gate Lake – New Brunswick

https://www.geodata.us/canada_names_maps/maps.php?featureid=DAJXY&f=35

Hell's Gate Lake is a real place in New Brunswick, situated at 46°54'25" North and 65°05'47" West, near St Margarets, North-East of Kouchibouguac National Park. Don't go there, please. It may or may not lead to Hell, but it's a really, really nasty place. In the dictionary, under muskeg, there's a picture of Hell's Gate Lake. Did I mention, don't go there?

Appendix 8

New Brunswick's 1840s Wolf Invasion

In 1830, a farmer called Barnabas Armstrong was nearly back to his farm when his sled was attacked by wolves. As he drove his horses madly to escape, his dog jumped off the wagon to fight the pack off. Barnabas got home, then returned with friends to find his dog. It was the first time wolves had been seen in New Brunswick. But it was not the last. In 1843, another farmer (Thomas Teeling) left his farm to get pork and beans. On his return he got chased for two miles by a pack of wolves. In 1844 a famous British author's camp was attacked by wolves. And the next Winter, attacks were reported at Lepreau River and Eel River Lake. A political party was formed with the sole platform of the destruction of bears and wolves, and the government upped the bounty for wolf pelts to a sum around four month's wages.

No wolves have been reported sighted in New Brunswick since 1862. By coincidence, that was when the government bounty ended. Some theories suggest the last wolves were wiped out in 1846, and the pelts delivered for bounty since then had been imported by unscrupulous hunters. Or maybe–just maybe–a new guardian and guide came to them, and guided them to forests and trails no hunter would ever find. Perhaps...

Appendix 9

Gamby – New Brunswick's 'frozen man'

Just before Christmas, in 1859, near the settlement of Chipman and near the Gaspereau river, a young man, apparently a young Italian of around nineteen, was found on a logging trail. His legs were quite literally frozen and paralysed, and although some people said they recognised him as having worked at a local sawyers he was never really identified. He was initially taken to Chipman, and cared for by various locals. But his legs got worse, and he was taken to a Doctor, who amputated them and sealed them with tar to save his life. During his surgery, he kept shouting something the Doctor recalled as 'Gamby' 'or 'Gamba' – Italian for leg. So his nickname became Gamby. He was taken back to Chipman, but the expenses of caring for him kept rising, and no local or federal money was made available for his care. And in 1863, a number of 'concerned locals' apparently found a solution. For the sum of twenty five pounds, they found a 'mysterious stranger' who offered to take him off their hands.

Gamby was never seen again.

NOTE:

More extensive treatments on the Great Wolf Invasion, Gamby and Jerome can be found at Andrew Maclean's Backyard History pages. My thanks for Andrew for putting up with me and tolerating my questions :-).

https://backyardhistory.ca/articles/f/wolf-attack

https://backyardhistory.ca/articles/f/the-legless-mystery-man

Graeme Smith books published by BWL Publishing

Much Ado About Dragons (The Book of the Idiot 1)
A Not-Summer Night's Scream (The Book of the Idiot 2)
Jack Shadow (Shadow Dance Book 1)
Shadow Child (Shadow Dance Book 2)
18 Wheels and No Roses (Road Like a River Book 1)

This is me–Graeme Smith. Professional liar. I tell people–readers, I mean–that things that never really happened actually did happen, and that they happened to people who don't really exist. And, if I do it right, for a while, even if just for a moment (or a page, a chapter, a book)? Well, they believe me. Readers, I mean. They believe. Heck, if I'm lucky, if they bought one of my books, I get paid to lie to them! Samuel Taylor Coleridge (who got to be famous, at least in part, by not even <u>finishing</u> a lie) called it the 'suspension of disbelief'. He thought it was a Good Thing(tm). Tolkien–dragons and hobbits and elves, oh my–thought it wasn't. He believed in 'secondary belief' and thought suspension of belief was for wusses. But really, that's what authors–fiction authors–are. Professional liars. Well, the ones who manage the 'getting paid' thing are :-).

So here we are. This is me–Graeme Smith, Fantasy author. Time was, I worked on a psychiatric ward. Now I write about people who believe in magic and dragons, and who live where the folk who *don't* are the ones who need help :-). Welcome to my worlds! Sit down, pull up a chair–and I'll lie to you some :-).

9 780228 636823